PRAISE FOR *RATTLESNAKE RODEO*

"Nick Kolakowski is known for his insightful essays on complex social issues and controversies within the world of crime fiction but, for those unfamiliar with his fiction, *Rattlesnake Rodeo* (and its fantastic predecessor, *Boise Longpig Hunting Club*) are terrific starting points. At turns ruthless and intimate, but always with a touch of humor, *Rodeo* takes readers on a violent, memorable journey through the new American West and the dark violence plaguing his characters' souls."

—E.A. Aymar, author of *The Unrepentant*

RATTLESNAKE RODEO

BOOKS BY NICK KOLAKOWSKI

The Boise Longpig Hunting Club Series
Boise Longpig Hunting Club
Rattlesnake Rodeo

The Love & Bullets Series
A Brutal Bunch of Heartbroken Saps
Slaughterhouse Blues
Main Bad Guy

Somebody's Trying to Kill Me (and Other Stories)
Maxine Unleashes Doomsday
Finest Sh*t! (and Other Stories)

NICK KOLAKOWSKI

RATTLESNAKE RODEO

To Arlie, Jared, and Laika—for the adventures

PART 1
CLEANUP

1

After we blew up a few of the richest and most powerful men in Idaho, my sister Frankie wanted to stop for fries. We had a plastic tub filled with charred phones and wallets in the back seat of our stolen SUV, three pistols under the front seats, an AK-47 in the cargo area, and yet she felt calm enough to steer us toward deep-fried carbs and probably too many eyewitnesses. Ever since we were kids, Frankie was always the weirder sibling.

"We got a lot to do if we want to stay upright and breathing," Frankie explained as she twisted the wheel, leaning into yet another mountain curve. "We'll need all the calories we can get."

In the back, my once-and-future wife Janine sorted through the bin, peeling melted driver's licenses and high-end credit cards from blackened leather. We had found these personal effects in a locked metal box thrown clear of the explosion. The men we killed had used that box to secure their personal effects before trying to hunt us down, like how I would put my wallet and phone in my gym locker before a monster weightlifting set. I felt zero remorse over converting those sick bastards into piles of charred hamburger.

"Maybe we should toss these phones out the window," Janine said. "Someone could track them, right?"

"We need to get whatever info off them we can," Frankie said. "Then we'll dump. There's no signal up here, anyway."

"I'm trying to find my phone right now, but there's a lot of scrap…" Janine held up a charred lump of plastic and bubbly glass.

The road dipped into a valley prickly with burned trees, its rocky sides plunging into a narrow river foaming with rapids. Even steeper mountains beyond, the ridges patched with snow. Under ordinary circumstances, I would have found the view peaceful, but my stomach was imploding, a black hole vacuuming up my body heat from the inside. When was the last time I had been this scared? Iraq?

We were dead. Although I didn't want to say it out loud, I knew that our life expectancy had almost certainly dropped to zero, no matter what we did or where we went. When you carbonize a group of millionaires, politicians, and millionaire-politicians, the law never stops hunting you, and they make sure you'll never have the chance to say something embarrassing at trial.

No. We would get through this. We had to.

We had a daughter who deserved to live. I took a deep breath, held it, and exhaled, feeling a little calmer. My side-view mirror framed the pickup with Frankie's men, trailing a hundred yards behind, and that helped my mood, too. No matter what the odds, we had Frankie's crew and whatever information we could pull from these charred phones. We had my experience as a soldier and bounty hunter, combined with Frankie's considerable experience in doing terrible things to other human beings for money.

The satellite phone in Frankie's lap buzzed, and she answered it one-handed. "What?" She listened for a few moments before ending the call. Smiling, she said: "My boys."

"What's that?" I asked.

"We got a little surprise at Redfish Lake. Maybe a good one." She stomped the gas, bucking the SUV forward. "And they got that restaurant, right? At the lodge? Excellent fries."

Once upon a time, the story goes, Redfish Lake teemed with so many salmon that the water gleamed red. Hence the name. The fish were long gone, but it was a popular place to party.

Before we had our kid, Janine and I would drive up from Boise to bike the rocky trails and hang out with our friends on the water. "It's Saturday," I said. "Big crowd, lot of witnesses. Maybe a concert or two later. You think this is a good idea?"

Frankie cocked an eyebrow. "My IQ didn't suddenly drop by fifty points, bro. Trust me."

A phone beeped, and Janine said: "This idiot's code was one-two-three-four-five. I'm serious."

"Who's the idiot?" I asked, spinning around to face her.

Janine tapped the shattered screen a few times. "Oh shit, it's Ted Ryan."

"Senators," Frankie said, "aren't exactly known for being a bright species."

"See if you can find anything incriminating," I offered. "Any leverage is good leverage, even after someone's dead."

"He better not have any goat porn on this thing," Janine said, swiping through images. "If I'm mentally scarred, you're the one who'll have to deal with it."

"I'll keep it in mind," I said. Truth be told, I was glad that Janine was joking. A few hours ago, she had killed a man. The first time I ended someone's life, I vomited my guts out, but she seemed pretty okay so far.

"No porn. Just, ah, a lot of food shots," Janine said. "Maybe he's got a second phone for his erotic barnyard thrills." Tossing the device into the bin, she wiped her hands on her jeans, leaving faint, sooty smears, and tapped her kneecaps in a familiar rhythm: two fast, three slow. She stopped after that, which was another positive sign. Despite the stress of the past day, her OCD appeared under control, maybe suppressed by the shock and adrenaline.

I drifted a hand around her ankle and squeezed. She bent down, took my hand in both of hers, and squeezed back.

It was another forty-five minutes of high-speed driving to reach the lake. Turning off the main road, we found ourselves on a narrow drive made narrower by the trucks and cars parked in the ditches on either side. Picture-perfect families pushed strollers and toted colorful canoes in the direction of the still-unseen lake. For the first time since Frankie had pressed the button on the detonator that blew those powerful men to little bits, I wondered how we looked to strangers.

If we were lucky, the happy civilians slipping past our windows would assume we were hikers at the end of a long trip: dusty, exhausted, more than a little ragged around the edges. If we were unlucky, some paranoid mother would think we were vagrants looking to rob a few minivans. I had zero urge to explain myself to any cops or private security. Were fries really worth all this? What was this fabulous surprise that Frankie's men had for us?

The drive opened onto a parking lot, and we slid into an empty slot behind a wooden maintenance shed. The pickup with Frankie's men rumbled past, on the hunt for another spot. Turning off the engine, scanning the mirrors for anything suspicious, Frankie reached under her seat and pulled out one of the pistols hidden there, an M1911. She pressed the slide forward enough to verify a round in the chamber before lifting her hips and sliding the gun into her waistband. "My kingdom for a holster," she said, grinning.

I knew how she felt. Jamming two or three pounds of metal next to your ass for a sustained amount of time is often uncomfortable, and the barrel has a nasty tendency to tangle in your underwear.

I reached beneath my own seat and retrieved a 9mm pistol, its frame plated with gold. I had found it on the ground after we killed everyone up north, and as much as I hated these flashy pistols that rich idiots sometimes bought, it was preferable to the third handgun in the vehicle, a short-barreled Ruger Super Redhawk that only held five rounds. Stuffing it down the back of my jeans—my kingdom for a holster, indeed—I booted open my door and climbed out.

The pickup had found a spot fifty yards from us, behind a small dirt mound that separated the parking lot from the brown-sand beach. Four of Frankie's men stood beside the rear bumper: thickly bearded, dressed in black-and-blue windbreakers, their heads masked by sunglasses and baseball caps. While they all appeared unarmed at first glance, they no doubt had enough weaponry strapped to their bodies to fight a small-scale war.

I walked toward them on legs that felt weak, shaky. Exhaustion had left me a hollowed-out shell. The only cure was fifteen hours of shut-eye, but until I could find a safe bed, I would need to gorge on food to power through.

One of Frankie's men, a redheaded bruiser named Benedict, stepped forward, his hand extended. "Good to see you, partner," he said.

"Likewise." We shook, and I pulled him in for a hug. Benedict had worked for Frankie for years, often driving loads of guns between Idaho and the Mexican border. The bottom half of his unruly beard was cinched with a rubber band, keeping it somewhat tamed. He was half Cherokee on his mother's side and proud of it.

"Sounded like you messed some folks up real good," Benedict said.

"That's right," I replied. The beach appeared empty of civilians. Two bright white boats drifted near the dock, loaded with sunburnt people cheering their own drunkenness. To our left, on the wide lawn between the main lodge and the water, the small stage where musicians would perform their greatest hits stood empty. We still had a few hours before evening fell and the concerts kicked off, drawing the day's biggest crowds.

"Where's my surprise?" Frankie asked, walking up behind me.

"You look like you had a hell of a night," Benedict told her.

"Yeah, it was the polar opposite of fun, which is making me very, very impatient. My surprise?"

"We rented a cabin," Benedict said, jutting his chin toward the trees behind us. "Little bit of isolation. In case things get loud."

By this point, Janine had joined us. I noted the bulge beneath her loose T-shirt: the Ruger Super Redhawk. The Janine of even a day ago would never have dreamed of packing a pistol. Our lives had changed forever, and not for the better.

"Come on." Benedict started across the lot, waving for us to follow.

"Get us some food," Frankie told one of the other men, a blonde surfer-type with a scar slashing his left cheek. "Fries, burgers, chips, everything you can carry. We're feeding everyone."

"Anyone got dietary issues?" Surfer Boy asked us. "Gluten-free? It's okay if you are."

Benedict's eyebrows rose above his sunglasses. "Cut it out with that shit."

Surfer Boy shrugged. "Trying to be accommodating, man..."

"Meet us in the cabin," Frankie said, gesturing for Benedict to lead off. As we crossed the parking lot, Janine tap-tap-tap-tapped the pistol grip through her shirt. I reached over and squeezed her hand. Things might have changed, but we were still here, still together.

The cabins, scattered in the woods behind the main lodge, had nice curtains of trees to block the view from the road and the parking lots. Ours had a dusty SUV parked behind it, with another of Frankie's men leaning against the hood. Someone had piled several bags of laundry in the SUV's front passenger seat—or at least I thought it was laundry until I came closer. The pile had a swarthy face, eyes closed and mouth open. Through the smeared windows, we heard faint snoring. The man on the hood waved as Benedict unlocked the cabin door and held it open for us.

"Welcome to your new home away from home," Benedict said. We entered an efficiency kitchen that opened onto a living room with a small couch, a coffee table stacked with board games and children's books, and a few wooden chairs. Thick curtains covered the windows, but a small lamp in the far corner cast a circle of yellow light on a large, scruffy man tied to one of the chairs.

"Hey, everything you need for a fantastic weekend in the woods," I said. "Stove, shower, comfortable seating, and a hostage for when things get boring."

"Who's this guy?" Frankie asked, walking over to the captive.

"We hit Ted Baker's house, just like you told us," Benedict said. "Everybody had cleared out, but we found him in the basement. It's Baker's nephew. His name is Keith."

"Hey, Keith," Frankie said, leaning down until she entered the man's sightline.

"I am not a god," Keith said, tilting his head upward. His eyes drifted, unfocused. "I am a poet."

"You hit him too hard?" Janine asked Benedict. "Why's he babbling?"

Benedict shrugged. "When they found him, he was eating a whole bag of weed brownies. Strong shit, too. You know Little Bubba, he's like four hundred pounds, but he took a little nibble off one of them and it knocked him right out. He's still in the car out there. And that's not even the weirdest part."

Closing her eyes, Frankie squeezed the bridge of her nose with two fingers. "Try me."

"Keith here, he used to be a cop in Boise. We found a bunch of photographs in his room, along with a ton of old documents. He got booted off the force."

"Let me guess," Frankie said. "Drug use?"

"I told them that I see to the very edges of the known universe, into the face of Deep Time itself," Keith informed us. "They didn't dig that very much."

"Boise PD is no place for philosophy," I said. When I wasn't fighting for my life in the woods of Idaho, I was a bounty hunter, which meant I dealt with the police several times a week. John Q. Public might have thought of cops as pretty much all the same, macho types who loved pumping weights and cracking skulls. I knew they were often much more: I'd met intellectuals who loved books, burnouts who wanted to retire so they could fish (I understood that impulse), not-so-secret psycho-paths who wanted to bring the pain, angels hungry to serve and protect. I had never met a cop anywhere close to Keith's level of drugged-out space alien, so I guessed at some point he had been sober, and likely quite different. What had happened to him?

I stepped to one side, for a better angle on Keith's doughy face. Although his family had more money than anyone in Idaho, Keith evidently opted to cut his own hair, leaving a spectacular bald patch on his scalp. His chin was shaven clean, transforming his beard into a pair of mismatched mutton chops. He looked exhausted, the chemicals in his blood forcing his organs to work overtime.

"Keith, come back to Earth for a minute." Frankie snapped her fingers under his nose. "We need to talk. Do you know who I am?"

Keith's eyes brightened. "You're Hel, the goddess of death."

"Yep, close enough. Keith, you remember the game your uncle liked to play?"

Keith pouted. "He played lots of games. Mean ones, sometimes. Once, he took my special weed, my Purple Crush, and told me that I'd only get it back if I ate one of his turds from the toilet, so I did. It was *warm*."

"Well, that sounds marvelously entertaining, but I'm referring to the one where your brother and his rich friends kidnapped people, drove them up into the mountains, and hunted them for sport. You remember that one?"

Keith nodded.

"Good." Frankie leaned forward. "I know we haven't exactly caught you at your best moment—sorry about that—but I need you to tell me about anyone who helped your uncle arrange that game, okay? Anything is helpful."

"The game…" Keith coughed, snot bubbling from his nostrils. "It takes place in Eden. A thousand years in Eden, where Karen is. You can't outlast Karen."

"Who is Karen?"

"Karen is a bigger Hel, a more complete goddess. She drives a Mercedes that shoots bubbles."

Frankie placed her fingers on Keith's windpipe, her nails dimpling his flesh. "You're going to have two options here. Option one: I drug you with something that paralyzes you from the neck down, place you in a bathtub, get the water running, and step away to take a very long phone call. It'll take at least a half-hour for you to finally drown, and you'll spend most of that coughing water. Option two, which I like to call 'speedy service,' is I just rip out your tongue through your neck. Either of those appeal to you?"

Keith squeaked like a frightened mouse but made no attempt to pull away. I had a flashback to another dusty hotel room, my sister jamming a shotgun into my neighbor's face and pulling the trigger. If Keith's addled mind refused to spit up anything useful, she might kill him on the spot. I wondered, not for the first time, whether Frankie was becoming a little too blood-thirsty for her own good.

"Keith," I said, stepping closer to the chair. "Did your uncle have a safe? Someplace he kept his special stuff?"

"When they searched the house," Benedict said behind me, "they took some laptops and other things. No safes that we found, but it's a big place."

"Baker's sensitive stuff, it probably wasn't in the house," I said. "He was evil, but he wasn't dumb." To my immense relief, Frankie removed her fingers from Keith's throat. The scruffy lunatic had no idea how close he'd come to seeing a chunk of his windpipe before he died.

"My uncle's got an office, not that big building in Boise, another one." Keith shook his head, snorting back a fresh load of snot. "It's got no light, no color, only a big black hole."

"You ever been inside?" I asked. "Where is it?"

As soon as I asked the question, I tensed, ready for Keith to offer directions to Mars. Instead, he named an address along Federal Way, a long strip of storage units, RV sales lots, and warehouses punctuated by dry fields. Then he settled back, his gaze fogging. "I'm a creature of light, man," he muttered. "No black holes for me."

I turned to Frankie. "We ought to check there. Anything useful, we can use it to hold off Baker's friends, partners, whoever."

"Some of Baker's stuff survived the blast," Janine said. "There was a key card in his wallet. It was melted a bit, but I bet it'll still work."

Frankie told Benedict: "Keep at least two guys here, with Keith. He's got some worth as a bargaining chip."

"I shoot golden beams," Keith offered. "My value to the universe is immense."

Still looking at Benedict, Frankie said: "Where's the Monkey Man?"

"Stayed behind in Boise. He led the raid on Baker's house."

"Have him meet us out on Federal Way tonight. They searched that house top to bottom, right?"

"That's right."

"And nobody was there except for Keith?"

Benedict shook his head.

"Okay. Then have the Monkey Man burn it down. Make sure he does it so nothing around the property goes up. I don't want to be responsible for starting a wildfire."

Keith's chin had slumped to his chest, his eyes closed. Frankie was usually careful about discussing business in front of potential witnesses, and I wondered if she thought Keith was too blazed to rat us out to any cops. Either that, or she planned on killing him once his potential value ran out.

The front door opened, and Surfer Boy entered, his arms loaded with paper trays filled with fries, chips, and a dozen burgers and hot dogs. He set the food on the counter, wiped his hands on his hips, and said: "Someone owes me forty bucks."

"I'll give you eighty in a bit," Frankie said. "Bills might be a little scorched, though."

"Works for me. Bennie, I got you a burger without a bun.

Gluten-free, you know?"

"Cram it up your ass," Benedict said, struggling to repress a smile.

After handing Janine a hot dog, I stripped the greasy paper away from a double-patty burger and devoured it in three bites. My stomach demanded more, so I followed up with a handful of fries slathered in ketchup. When Frankie arched an eyebrow, passing judgment on my gluttony, I offered her a wolfish growl.

"Table manners," Frankie said, adopting a prim English accent, "are what separate the beasts from the humans, my dear."

Janine handed her a bag of fries. "Is it hunger making you talk like the queen?"

Winking at me, Frankie shoved every fry from the bag into her mouth, chewing until her cheeks bulged. Everyone laughed except Keith, who snorted and said: "You're all done in the sunlight."

Our laughter died.

"Karen's going to come down from Eden and slaughter you all." Keith smiled, revealing yellowed teeth. "She's going to put your heads on pikes, on the border of heaven. You won't be dead, though. Your severed heads, they're gonna scream..."

Setting down her empty fry bag on the counter, Frankie walked over to the coffee table and sorted through the stack of children's books beside the board games. On the bottom was a thick hardcover titled *This Big Friendly World!* Frankie pulled it free, testing its balance, giving Keith another few moments to rant about angels and heaven and heads.

When Keith paused for breath, she spun on her heel, arms rising, and slammed the book into his face. A tooth flickered across the room, ricocheting off a wall before disappearing behind the couch. Keith yelped and fell backward, still tied to the chair.

"I don't know anything about Eden," Frankie told him. "But if you don't shut up for the rest of the day, you're getting option one. You hear me?"

Smacked sober, Keith spat blood and nodded.

2

I was proud of Frankie. Rather than murder Keith, she had only cracked his jaw. On the three-hour drive to Boise, we said little, our attention locked on the radio crackling news reports every twenty minutes. No word of famous people disappearing, or shootouts in the woods. During the hunt, we had set part of an abandoned town on fire, and I supposed that smoke from the inferno would eventually alert some hikers and rangers. Even then, it might take days for the broader world to realize the true extent of the chaos.

Every few miles, I glanced in the side mirror. Benedict followed us in the SUV, Surfer Boy beside him, Little Bubba still passed out in the back seat. They were wired for combat (well, except Bubba), but I doubted anyone would hit us on the road. As my father told me once, you're safe when you're traveling fast. It's when you stop that you need to worry.

"Baby, I found our devices. You had a red case on your iPhone, right?" Janine held up a melted bit of red plastic, a blackened sliver of aluminum and circuit-board embedded in its center. "Some of these scraps could be my phone, too."

I hissed through clenched teeth. "That sucks."

"This is for the truck, right?" She tossed me a key, slightly bent, its fob reduced to a gray lump.

I turned it over in my hands. "Um, maybe?"

"Probably still works. Also found your wallet, so that's a big

14

win." She handed over a scorched lump of leather and plastic.

Opening it, I found that my driver's license had survived, along with one of my credit cards, but the rest was unrecognizable. "Yeah, look at all this winning," I said, stuffing the mess in my pocket.

"Back to snooping." Fetching a somewhat-intact phone from the bin, she held down the power button until the bubbled screen lit up, filling the back seat with a white glow.

"I'm just glad we're in one piece, baby." My voice was a little shakier than I liked.

"Yeah, but I could use a massage." She tapped in a code, then another. "Guess what? This guy's password is zero-zero-zero-zero. I didn't even realize phones let you use that anymore."

"Whose phone is it?" I asked.

"Hold on." Janine flicked through the contacts. "Jeff Hart? Who's that?"

"No idea."

"He's an heir to something," Frankie said. "Like, box stores or something. Look him up."

"Honestly, I'd rather call my daughter." Janine shook the phone. "But it'd be a bad idea to do that from this one, right? They'd sure trace that."

"That's right," Frankie said.

"Should have asked one of your men for their phone." Tossing the device into the bin, Janine flopped back in her seat, wiping her hands on her pants, tapping her knees. Based on the speed of the taps, I could tell that thinking about our daughter had spiked her stress levels.

"Not a great idea, either," Frankie said. "In the meantime, if you could turn off any phones that are still on, that'd be great. We're closer to constant coverage, so someone could start tracking. I'm still not sure what I want to do with all those things."

"The phones and wallets?" I said. "We totally need to get rid of them."

"Maybe. It's also a treasure trove, if it's used right. My people could spend days mining the data on them."

"Sure, if a SWAT team doesn't kick in your door, first."

"I'd like to see them get past my redneck security system." Frankie returned her attention to the road.

"What's a redneck security system?" Janine asked.

"Twenty landmines deployed across my lawn," Frankie said. It was hard to tell if she was joking.

We stayed quiet for another forty miles, through another news update that focused on football scores and the president's latest lunacy, followed by nothing but faint static as we dipped through another long valley. A sign for a hot spring snapped past, followed by a gas station with old-style pumps beneath a blue awning—the first sign of civilization in at least an hour, and a familiar one. Years ago, on any road trip that took us down Highway 55, Frankie and I would stop there for beers and ice cream.

Frankie's distant gaze hinted at her own trip down memory lane. She said, more to Janine than me: "When I first started out, I was running guns to guys in Juárez. Small-time crews, not the cartels, which didn't need some chick to sell them secondhand nines and forty-fives. It wasn't fantastic money, given the risk, but I was twenty-two and trying to make a name for myself."

"You were buying from those guys in Oregon, right?" I asked. "And driving them south, over the border?"

"That's right. Remember my old Volvo with the compartment under the floorboards? Aw, I miss that car so much. Anyway, one day I arrive in Juárez, ready to do some business, but my guys are nowhere to be found, and nobody's saying anything. I'm pissed because I just drove these rifles through a couple of checkpoints. So I make some calls, and I'm sitting in a little restaurant with awesome burritos, waiting for any kind of response. And a man walks in."

This wasn't a story I knew.

"He was a well-dressed guy," Frankie continued, "in a white

suit and a white hat. Middle-aged, kind of fat, with this gray moustache. I thought about making a joke about the Mexican Colonel Sanders, but I stopped when I got a good look at his eyes, which were as dead as a stuffed animal's. He took a seat at my table, and I could tell he was unarmed. I had my hand in my jacket pocket, on the little pistol I kept there, but I knew if I used it, I would never leave Juárez alive. The man was from the cartel."

"Which one?" I asked.

"To this day, I don't know. He kept saying 'my employer' in this whispery little voice. His employer didn't have a problem with me, he said, but there was a problem with the guys I sold guns to. He told me that they'd been liquidated, those guys, but that I was free to come and go in Juárez, provided I never sold a weapon there again."

"That's quite a story."

"That's not everything. As he was getting up to leave, I did a stupid thing. I asked him, 'What's the secret of success?' Like I was still a college student, and he was a professor, and I was looking for life advice. I swear, it slipped out. Shows how young I was."

"What'd he say?" Janine asked.

"To his credit, he didn't have me killed on the spot for being an idiot. Instead, he smiled and said: 'Theatricality will get you everywhere.' It pissed me off at first, because I didn't understand what he meant, but before I could ask him anything else, he left the restaurant. I finished my burrito, got back in the Volvo, and headed for the border. Traffic was slow. At first, I thought it was because of an accident. Then I saw the real reason why." Frankie swallowed. "There was a crime scene. By shitty coincidence, it was my guys, the ones I sold guns to. The cartel had decapitated them and set the heads on this low stone wall by the road, then hung the bodies from an overpass right across. That was what the man meant by theatricality. Freak everyone out, and they're too scared to come at you."

A few months ago, Frankie might have told that story at one of our backyard barbeques, and Janine might have retaliated by refusing to invite her over for a month or two. The old Janine disliked tales of murder and gore. Heck, she usually refused to watch action movies, which meant I put on a classic John Woo flick and blasted it loud whenever I was feeling passive-aggressive and wanted her out of the house. Now the same woman leaned between the seats, locked on Frankie's words.

"And for a long time, I thought that was the right strategy," Frankie said. "You blow up an enemy with a rocket launcher, it sends a message that you'll always escalate, no matter what the situation. You let your main guy wear a rubber monkey mask, it tells folks you're a little bit crazy. But I've been having second thoughts. Even before this crap we just went through, I had the FBI on my ass. Maybe a big show isn't always a great idea."

"We're going to have to lie low for a long time after all this, anyway," I said.

"That's true." Frankie sighed. "I've been thinking about retirement."

That startled me: my sister was an adrenaline junkie, and as much as I feared for her safety, I could never see her quitting her life as an arms dealer. What was she going to do instead, paint cornfields like Van Gogh?

"Not that I can retire," Frankie continued. "Too much overhead, too many people depending on me. I'd need a big score."

"Have you ever thought about going legit?" Janine asked. "Like, open a gun store or something?"

Frankie winced. "Boring. Plus, I hate paying taxes."

"Before we plan big scores," I said, "we should focus on cleaning up the current mess. Chances that Karen's a real person?"

"Pretty good, but Keith's brain is an egg frying on a skillet. Karen could be the lady at his local coffee place who refuses to listen to his crackpot theories on the Illuminati. And if some crazy bitch does pop out of the woodwork, we'll handle her." Frankie flashed her fangs at me. "Probably not with a rocket launcher, though."

For the first time in many miles, we slowed, approaching the turnoff that led through a rocky notch into the Treasure Valley. Down below, Boise awaited us. I thumbed the dashboard vent, angling it away from me, but the coldness I felt had nothing to do with the temperature in the car. Frankie seemed so confident, and yet I sensed an evil rushing down like the night out of the east, a deep blackness that would drown us.

3

At the rear of a parking lot for RVs, the Monkey Man waited for us in a battered red van. He leaned forward in the driver's seat, sunk in shadow, an unlit cigarette poking from the mouth of the weird rubber gorilla mask I had never seen him remove. As we climbed in, I wondered—for the thousandth time—where Frankie had found such a strange soul. Whenever I asked about his origins, she merely shrugged and smiled.

After a long pause to study his mask, Janine slid into the seat directly behind the Monkey Man, glancing at me once for reassurance. I nodded, realizing that I had never mentioned Frankie's weirdest lieutenant to her.

"Don't get too settled in," Frankie told us as she climbed into the front seat. Turning to the Monkey Man, she said: "You got it?"

Nodding, the Monkey Man fished in the hip pocket of his gray jumpsuit and retrieved a cheap phone. Frankie took the device and gave it to Janine. "It's clean," Frankie said. "Call the kid. Stay behind that RV in front of us, so nobody will see the light."

"I want to talk to her, too," I said as Janine tumbled out of the van, her fingers blurring over the numbers. Raising a hand in acknowledgment, Janine disappeared behind the RV, her voice softening like it always did when she talked to our daughter. I figured we had five minutes before she returned.

Meanwhile, Frankie angled her head to the Monkey Man so

he could whisper in her ear. When he finished, she straightened, turned to me, and said: "A bunch of people went into the target building an hour ago."

"That building, can we see it from here?" I asked.

The Monkey Man pointed through the windshield. I followed his finger to a narrow gap cut in the sagging chain-link fence that bordered the parking lot. Beyond lay a wide field, thick with knee-high weeds. At its far end rose a squat black box of a building, free of signs or lights. When Keith rambled about a black hole, he wasn't kidding.

"Here," Frankie said, tapping something hard against my forearm: a night-vision scope, an expensive one with internal focusing, which I raised to my left eye. I wished I had one of these things to shoot the occasional rattlesnake that lurked too close to my house, but Janine kept a tight rein on the household budget. Ammunition might have been a necessary expense, along with the occasional firearm upgrade, but my wife regarded things like scopes as luxuries when we had a mortgage to pay.

The scope transformed the nighttime murk into green-tinted daylight. I swept it along the roof of the building, then the field. No people in sight. What kind of idiots didn't set a perimeter?

"Maybe it's not a trap," I said. "More like a cleaning crew."

"Anyone come back out?" Frankie asked the Monkey Man, who shook his head.

"If they're cleaning," I said. "They know Baker is dead. Unless Keith called someone before you nabbed him."

"I doubt it. Keith was floating halfway to Jupiter when they hit the house. Cleaning crew or no, the Monkey Man says they had a couple of sidearms."

"Nothing we can't handle. How many more men do we have?"

"I told Benedict to park with his guys maybe half a mile down the road, on the other side. Bubba's over his weed coma by now, hopefully, or Benedict will jam a pencil in his ear until he wakes up. Three other guys at the intersection back there, a mile or so." Frankie jerked a thumb over her shoulder.

I handed back the night-vision scope. "Baker's house burn okay?"

The Monkey Man offered a vigorous thumbs-up before leaning over to whisper in Frankie's ear again. She barked laughter, her eyes widening in surprise. "No," she said to him. "No, you didn't."

The Monkey Man leaned back in his seat, his fingers drumming a jaunty tune on the steering wheel.

"Before they torched it all up, they raided the wine cellar." Frankie paused to press the back of her hand against her mouth, stifling another burst of the giggles. "Get out, take a look in the back."

Exiting the van, I paused to check Janine's position. She crouched against the side of the RV, a silhouette except for the curve of her face lit softly by the phone screen. She smiled at whatever our daughter was saying, and I felt such an intense burst of love it made my knees quake. Things are going to be okay, I told myself. We'll make it through, if only because of that love.

The Monkey Man had left the van's rear doors propped open. In the small cargo area, I found a Remington pump-action shotgun and three Heckler & Koch UMP45 submachine guns, along with cardboard cartons of 12-gauge shells and .45 ammunition. The weapons were probably from Frankie's personal stash—she was a big fan of submachine guns with lighter bodies and considerable stopping power—but the dusty wine cases beyond the ammo cartons had definitely come from Baker's house.

"You're insane," I said, bending to read the labels on the cases. My knowledge of wines was pretty much nonexistent, but I assumed that "Domaine de la Romanée-Conti 1990" was an absurdly expensive vintage, given Baker's wealth and taste.

"Only the best," Frankie called back, and chuckled again. "I looked it up. They're worth twenty thousand dollars a bottle, or something."

"You should figure out how to store this properly. It spoils, right? Or doesn't it?"

"I'm going to sell it so fast, your head will spin. Although I might keep a few bottles for the guys. We can mix it with Diet Coke. I bet that'd be pretty good."

"Don't do that in front of a wine expert. Their head will explode right off their shoulders."

"I'd dig that. Bring the UMPs when you come back up, okay? And those flash suppressors behind the ammo. We might as well go in."

I did as asked, and the Monkey Man and Frankie climbed out of the van to prep the weapons. As she attached the night-vision scope to the frame of her rifle, Frankie said: "I know some purists hate this gun, because they think it's not controllable on full auto, but maybe they shouldn't be shooting on full auto. It's easy to learn how to operate, which is what most of my clients want."

"I bet most of your clients can't read," said Janine behind me. "Dear, our kid wants to talk."

I took the phone from her, my heart speeding. "Heya, sprout," I said, disappearing behind the same RV that Janine had used.

"Hey, Daddy." Kelly sounded tired, and why not? It was close to her bedtime.

"Whatcha up to?"

"Grandma and I made cookies. Then we watched *Frozen*."

"Haven't you seen that movie five hundred times?"

She giggled. "No, Daddy. Only four hundred times. What are you doing?"

"Watching *Frozen*."

She laughed harder. "No, you're not."

"You're right, I'm not. I'd never watch *Frozen* except with you. We're hanging out with Aunt Frankie."

"I miss you." The lonely note in her voice was impossible to miss.

I swallowed. "I know, baby. But I'll see you soon, okay?"

"Okay." She sighed. "Want to talk to grandma?"

"No, that's okay. Tell her I said 'hi.'" I loved my mother, but she would ask too many innocent questions about my day, and the prospect of lying to her made me uncomfortable.

"Okay. I love you, Daddy."

"I love you, too, sprout. I'll call you tomorrow, okay?"

"Okay. Bye, Daddy." A beep as Kelly ended the call.

I handed the phone to Frankie, thinking about my mindset on the drive to Redfish Lake. How my fear and exhaustion had threatened to drown any urge to survive. My daughter had no idea what was happening, but she had given me a gift nonetheless. I felt reenergized, determined to end this crisis on my terms. These people tried to take me away from my kid forever.

"Give me that," I said, gesturing for one of the rifles that Frankie had balanced against the van's wheel well.

"Safety's off, one in the pipe," she said, as I slotted the weapon against my shoulder, barrel pointed at the ground, testing the weight.

"Kicks like a mule, right?" I engaged the safety. I never understood those yahoos who left the safety off at all times.

"Kicks like a gun with appropriate stopping power," she corrected me, before turning to Janine. "I know you're a badass bitch, but we'd all feel more comfortable if you stayed behind."

"By myself?" Reaching under her shirt, Janine drew her new pistol and pressed it against her hip.

"For a few minutes, until we clear," I said. "And if anything goes wrong…"

Janine took a deep breath, her fingers flexing on the pistol grip. "Drive away? Try to cowboy my way through? How well is that going to work?"

"We're coming back," Frankie said, marching toward the fence and the field beyond, the Monkey Man on her heels. "If you want something to handle your nerves, there's a lot of wine in the back of the van."

"If I have any wine," Janine said, "I'll fall right asleep. We've been up for a day and a half, remember?"

I cupped the back of Janine's neck, brought her close, and pressed my lips to hers. She opened up, tongue probing my teeth. When I pulled away, she grabbed my hand and tapped one of her patterns into my palm, five quick jolts, like a spell to protect me. I figured I needed all the help I could get.

4

God's honest truth, Frankie's story about Juárez and the Mexican Colonel Sanders surprised me. I knew about the gunrunning, of course. Despite her fondness for wearing all black and killing anyone who crossed her, my sister could slip into a stunning impersonation of a bubbly airhead, a disguise she always used in those days to slip past the bored guards at border crossings. Yet she had kept the encounter with the cartel to herself, maybe because she thought it made her look weak, or maybe because she thought I'd worry too much about the implications.

You're the worst worrywart, Frankie liked to tell me. *You can never just have a plan. It's always contingency this, contingency that.*

She was right. Long before I joined the Army, I couldn't walk into a bar for a friendly beer on a Friday night without plotting my potential escape routes, on top of judging the room to see who might pose a threat. Our daddy, a pure and honest lawman, had taught me well.

Daddy was terminated by the Ada County Sheriff's Office for mouthing off to his superior. That was the official reason, at least. The real reason was a gunfight near the Lucky Peak Reservoir that resulted in the deaths of three cocaine smugglers from Juárez. The cocaine disappeared from the evidence locker, and after Daddy threatened to tell the FBI about it, his superiors fired him with a warning to keep quiet or else. Had our daddy been single, with no children, he might have spoken up anyway—he was that kind of righteous man. But he had kids to think about, and so he took a job at a for-profit prison, where a crazy prisoner stabbed him to death.

The cartels must have known what happened. The trafficking network couldn't lose a gram of coke without word of it trickling south. When Frankie showed up in Juárez a few years later, why did they let her live, considering our daddy had cost them so much money?

Maybe they didn't know she was related. Frankie was always a good operator, very careful about building her fake identities. Or maybe they didn't care: she had nothing to do with the reservoir shootout, and besides, a dead American girl far from home can raise too many questions.

Our daddy's ghost haunted us for years. When the coke disappeared, it threw a big wrench in the plans of Robert Baker, a mid-level dealer who owed some bad folks a lot of cash. Without the shipment, he was broke, and they killed him. Robert's brother Ted, who later became the richest man in the state, never forgave our daddy for the role he played in that deal gone wrong. Ted and his friends would eventually host a game in which they hunted people in the woods, and one day they decided to force me, my sister, and my wife to play. Too bad they let us get our hands on some explosives.

The past is never dead, Faulkner once wrote. He was right. The past is alive, and it's always interested in burying you.

5

As we approached the fence, Frankie paused. Turning to the Monkey Man, she said: "Stay here, cover the flank."

The Monkey Man drew tall, his back stiff, his hand flexing on the grip of his rifle.

"It's okay," I said. "You're protecting Janine, too, and for that, I thank you."

The Monkey Man bowed slightly before disappearing into the darkness beside the van. Through the windshield, I spied a ghostly sliver of Janine's face, tucked low behind the dashboard. Did having her cocooned in a few tons of steel and glass ease the fear nibbling at my stomach? Of course not. It was just the furthest we could put her from harm's way at the moment.

Frankie pulled out her phone, dialed a number, and murmured a few commands. Returning it to her pocket, she seated the butt of her rifle against her shoulder and peered through the scope.

"We good?" I asked.

"Yeah." She stepped through the gap in the fence, careful to avoid the tangled wire and dry thorns.

I had to pick my way through the gap without the benefit of a night-vision scope, and I did so slowly, paranoid of a rusty wire slicing my flesh. Frankie squatted in the tall grass beyond, sweeping the rifle slowly across the field. "Took you long enough," she whispered.

"Well, pardon me to hell. I can't see in the dark."

"Grow better eyes."

"Where are your guys?"

Without lifting her gaze from the scope, Janine flicked her head to the right. The fence ran along the edge of the field for another fifty yards or so, until it merged with the lightless sky above Federal Way. A lone pair of headlights sliced across the road, disappearing beyond the black hulk of our target building.

"They'll park a hundred yards down, march back in," Frankie rose to a crouch. "We're going to intersect at the back. I don't see any security."

I thumbed my safety off before following her. We moved in relays, the tall grass whispering against our legs, and by the time we reached the deeper shadow of the building my back was cold and damp with sweat. My old patrol instincts kicked into gear and I felt sharp, but I had also been awake too many hours to count. I only hoped that, when the time came, I could react fast enough to any threats.

We crouched again, and Frankie clicked her tongue once. An answering click from the dark, followed by a dry rustle ahead of us. Benedict appeared around the edge of the building, tight against its wall, and I guessed Surfer Boy was right behind.

Frankie scanned the rear of the building with her scope. "Door, metal, deadbolt," she told me. "No camera, no alarm that I can see."

"How do we get through?" I nodded to Surfer Boy, who materialized behind Benedict with an AR-15 in his grip.

"Benedict has a breaching round in his gun," Frankie said, and clicked again.

Benedict stood and moved to the door, a short pump-action shotgun in his hands. A 12-gauge breaching round, fired downward between doorframe and doorknob, will disintegrate a lock mechanism without any ricocheting fragments. He assumed the position, and we stacked behind him, Frankie's hand on his shoulder, Surfer Boy's on mine.

Benedict fired.

The door burst inward.

And then everything went to hell.

They must have been standing right behind the door, ready to exit, when Benedict pulled the trigger. No sooner had the door opened when someone behind it opened fire, three shots that sent Benedict spinning to the side. He fell against Frankie, who sidestepped and fired into the dark doorway, someone shrieking in pain, another shot snapping past my head.

To our left, Surfer Boy swung wide, erupting in a high-pitched scream that sliced like a knife through the roar of gunfire. Holding his rifle at hip level, he sprayed the doorway with the entire clip, the barrel jittering wildly. When his weapon clicked empty, he popped the empty magazine and fumbled a new one from the hip pocket of his cargo pants, still screaming. Incredible lung capacity. When the fresh magazine clicked home, he unleashed another burst of fire through the doorway, but it was pointless: if anyone was still alive inside, they would have shot him during that slow reload.

Surfer Boy, gasping for breath, dropped his rifle and drew a pistol from his waistband.

Kneeling, I jabbed two fingers into Benedict's neck. He had a faint, rapid pulse. Moving my hand down his shoulders and chest, I felt warm wetness below the collarbone.

"Hurts like a mother," Benedict rasped, sounding bubbly but surprisingly strong.

"Surfer Boy," I said. "Get over here, pressure this wound."

Surfer Boy, holstering his pistol, followed my hands and pressed his shaking fingers over the hole. Benedict groaned and cursed, which I chose to take as an encouraging sign.

Rejoining Frankie, who had kept her rifle aimed at the doorway, I said: "Let's go."

"We're going to clear," Frankie told Surfer Boy. "Call for retrieval, okay?"

"Okay." His berserker rage dissipated, Surfer Boy sounded

small and scared.

"Now," Frankie snapped.

"Okay." One palm pressed over Benedict's wound, Surfer Boy fished his phone from his pocket and dialed a number. I hoped Little Bubba was sober enough to drive in the dark without running anyone over.

"Jake," Frankie said. "Let's finish this."

There are few things worse than entering a building filled with an unknown number of people who want to kill you. I had done it on hundreds of nights in Iraq, the fear crushing my lungs whenever we kicked in a new door. No matter how accurate your intel, anything could go wrong: a fighter tucked in a spider-hole behind a cupboard, a weapons cache beneath a kitchen rug rigged to explode.

I tried stepping in front of Frankie, intent on taking point, and she pushed me aside. "Beauty before age," she whispered, stepping forward. As much as I feared for her safety, I never doubted her fighting skill. Circling behind her, I tapped her shoulder to let her know I was ready.

Frankie darted through the doorway, and I followed. We stepped over three bodies piled on the threshold, stinking of blood and bowels loosened by death. They wore white coveralls, green plastic shoe covers, and blue surgical gloves. Frankie dispensed one shot each to their chests before kneeling down, patting them for anything useful. No identification, no wallets, no keys or trinkets—only .22 pistols.

Beyond the bodies stretched a long hallway, lit by the red glow of an exit sign at the far end. Beneath it, a metal door with a push bar. We approached it at a crouch. An engine roared behind us, followed by a door slamming, and Surfer Boy telling someone that they needed to get to a doctor, fast.

We paused until the vehicle left. Stepping back, Frankie pressed her heel against the push bar and eased the door open an inch. Bright light shot through the gap, forcing us to squint. She clicked her tongue and darted her head to the left.

31

I tightened my sweaty grip on my weapon. My kingdom for a pair of tactical gloves.

Taking a deep breath, Frankie kicked the door open and moved through, low and fast. I went to the right, my boots echoing on concrete. We entered a windowless space with a high ceiling, likely a former warehouse, its every inch illuminated by suspended LED lights.

The air stank of gasoline.

In the center of the otherwise-empty room, someone had crafted a mountain of trash: torn cardboard boxes, piles of shredded paper, smashed electronics, and cheap furniture. All of it soaked with fuel. Frankie circled to the other side of the mess. "Come here," she called. "Step carefully."

I joined her in front of a red plastic gas canister, a black box duct-taped to its side. On the side of the box, a digital timer counted down, passing the fifteen-minute mark as we watched.

"I guess I'm not the only one with ideas about burning buildings," Frankie said, pointing at the bottom of the pile. "See how they put that couch down there? That's some good kindling."

It was a ratty couch, upholstered in fake leather, with yellow foam spilling from long tears in the arms. Someone had set a stack of framed photographs atop one of the cushions; the top one featured men in hunting gear smiling for the camera, Baker in the middle. I bet the other folks were famous, but it was hard to tell faces at this distance, especially since most wore thick scarves and hats with flaps.

"Should we disarm this bomb?" I asked.

"We could. It looks pretty crude. They weren't expecting anyone to try and stop it. I don't think there's anything worth saving, though. Actually, wait." Slinging her rifle over her shoulder, she picked up a bottle of cheap whiskey that had rolled free of the pyre. Someone had taken the cap, but a few ounces of amber liquid sloshed in the bottom.

"I'm not in the mood," I said.

"We're not going to drink this, dumbass. Besides, it probably has some psycho's backwash in it. We'll need it later."

"For what?"

"Evidence suppression."

I was about to deliver a witty follow-up when a glimmer in the pile caught my eye. I stepped forward, taking care to set my feet flat so I wouldn't slip. The fumes were making me light-headed. I shoveled some soaked papers from the edge of an acrylic display box, the kind you might use to show off a medal or a miniature boat. Inside the box was a bright plastic kitten on a gold chain, the kind of cheap necklace a teenager with a taste for anime might wear.

I stepped to the left, spying another box beneath a mound of cardboard. I was reluctant to move too much stuff around—if metal struck metal, the resulting spark could fry us—but I could see inside the box by bending down.

"We should go soon," Frankie said. "I'm paranoid of cops."

She was right, of course. This stretch of Federal Way was desolate at night, but there was always the chance that someone had heard the gunfire and called the police. Before we left, though, I wanted to solve the mystery of these boxes. The second one held a car key attached to a comically oversized rabbit's foot.

"They're trophies," Frankie said quietly.

"What?"

She nodded to my right. "There's another one over there, underneath that office chair. See it? Purple shoe, chunky sole. The stuff in all these boxes, I bet it belonged to people they killed in the game."

I retreated to her, careful with my steps.

The timer on the canister hit eleven minutes.

"Do me a favor," Frankie said, "and pick up that drive to your right."

She pointed at a portable hard drive at the edge of the pile, its casing cracked in two places. Whoever smashed it had done a poor job. I took care to lift the drive straight up, paranoid about its sharp corners scratching the concrete like a match. The label on the front said it was one terabyte in size. Stuffing it as best I could into my hip pocket, I hurried to join Frankie, who was already halfway to the door, the bottle in her left hand.

"I think this was a clubhouse," she said in the hallway. "There were a couple gun cases in there, smashed up. Also a humidor."

"Pretty crappy clubhouse."

"They weren't going for fun and cozy. They just wanted a place to store their sick crap out of sight." As we stepped over the bodies in the doorway, Frankie drove a foot into a head. "One for the road, asshole."

"That's not very nice," I mock-chided her.

"Bite me."

Outside, the only sign of Benedict was a streak of blood on the concrete. Frankie upended the bottle and washed away the stain with whiskey. "Can't be too careful," she said.

"What?"

"Contaminating the sample, if the cops take one. Come on."

Returning to the van, we found Janine and the Monkey Man in the front seats, an open bottle of wine on the console between them. We plopped in the back, and the Monkey Man started the engine and twisted the wheel, taking us on a long arc around the parked RVs. After buckling up and engaging the safety on my rifle, I helped myself to a swig of wine, letting my head flop back on the headrest. It was so tempting to close my eyes and fall asleep, despite my sizzling nerves.

Beside me, Frankie reached into my pocket and yanked out the hard drive. Holding it up so the Monkey Man could see, she said: "We're going to need to crack this."

The Monkey Man spun the wheel again to send us through the front gate, bumping a hard right onto Federal Way. Behind us, red-and-blue lights pulsed on the horizon, but the van's engine was too loud to hear any sirens. By roaring along at eighty with the headlights off, we would hopefully clear the area without anyone noticing us.

"Went off twenty seconds ago," Frankie said, checking her watch.

"What did?" Janine asked.

In the night behind us flickered a tiny flame, no bigger than a lit match. It lengthened, clawing for the stars, before disappearing again. Up close, it must have been a real inferno. From this widening distance, though, Ted Baker's Boise Longpig Hunting Club vaporized without much drama.

6

As the Monkey Man took the exit off I-184 that dropped into downtown Boise, Frankie turned to me and said: "You ever been to the safe house out near Nyssa, on the Oregon side?"

"I don't think so."

"It's a real fortress. Nobody will touch us there."

"Is your fortress fancy enough to have Wi-Fi?" Janine asked. "I got to check in with work."

"Yeah, we'll have you use a VPN, hide your location." Frankie gestured for the Monkey Man to park on a deserted street. "Tell me something, bro: when they found that dead girl in your gun safe the other day? Why'd you flee to a *hotel*? It's, like, the most unsafe option."

"It was convenient," I said. "Plus, we took precautions."

Frankie shook her head. "Your bags in your room, we should leave them. You can always buy more stuff."

Janine tapped her knees. "That's my stuff we're talking about."

"Plus, my truck's still parked out front," I said. "Hopefully."

"If I'm stuck in a fortress for who knows how long, I want my books, my clothing, my other stuff." Janine's fingers drummed harder. "How long are we going to stay there, anyway?"

"At the safe house?" Frankie bit a thumbnail. "I'd be lying if I gave you a definitive answer. We'll try to make it quick. There's a lot of unknown unknowns we need to deal with, to quote that jackass Donald Rumsfeld."

The Monkey Man muttered something inaudible to everyone but Frankie, who laughed. "Yes, we'll order pizza," she said, pulling out her phone and scrolling through messages. "Doc thinks Benedict will make it. Won't pitch for pro baseball anytime soon, but he can still pull a trigger, so he's not ready for the glue factory quite yet."

"I'm going in." I opened my door a few inches.

Slipping her phone into her hip pocket, Frankie retrieved a pistol from the glove compartment and stuffed it down the front of her pants. "I'm coming with you. Overwatch."

"What's that mean?" Janine asked.

"Means I'm standing on the sidewalk outside, make sure nobody sneaks up on your darling husband while he's checking out. Let's move."

After the cops had removed the dead girl's body from my gun safe, Janine insisted that we stay at the Belle Rive, a boutique hotel on Main Street. At first, I resented the decision. With its steel and dark-wood highlights, and hipster eatery in the main courtyard, the joint struck me as far too pretentious. I was fine sleeping anyplace with clean mattresses and a reasonably hot shower. But Janine overrode me, arguing that she earned enough from her copyediting projects to cover a few nights at a nicer establishment. If we risked dark forces tearing our lives apart, she wanted easy access to good cocktails and premium toiletries.

"I'm coming with you," Janine said. "You'll need help carrying stuff."

"No," I said.

"She's right." Frankie opened her door. "If she gets the bags, that'll keep your hands free. Who knows what shit we're heading into."

As the three of us approached the Belle Rive, I could only conclude that Janine had made the right choice in accommodations, but not for the reasons she thought. The hotel was once a motor lodge, with rooms opening onto a balcony that wrapped around the second floor. I had an angle on every stairwell and approach to our room, and the path looked clear.

Frankie waited outside while we headed into the office on the ground floor. Our room keys had mostly melted, but I recognized the night clerk. "Hey," I said, forcing my lips into the cheeriest smile I could manage under the circumstances. "Lost my key at the bar. Could you make us a spare?"

"Sure," he said, pulling a blank key from a drawer. "Looks like you had kind of a rough night, partner. What was that room number?"

"Two-oh-eight."

"Okay." Slipping the key into a card reader on the desk beside him, he asked Janine: "You need one, too?"

"Nope," she said. "We're checking out after we get our stuff."

"Oh." He hesitated. "Do you want to check out now?"

"Sure." I fished my blackened credit card from my pocket. Hopefully the magnetic strip still worked.

The clerk made no move to take it.

"Hey, it was a rough night." I dropped the card between us. "We went to a house party and, um, the house caught on fire."

The clerk took a step backward.

"I bet I'm not the worst-off guest you've seen lately." I said. "Besides, my money's good. Capitalism, am I right?"

Sighing, the clerk picked up the card, holding it by his fingernails as he swiped it through the reader. "You're good to go," he said. "You want a receipt, or do you want us to email it to you?"

"Email is fine."

"Thank you for staying with us." The clerk handed the card back, along with a mint from a bowl beside his computer. "Try to avoid any house fires in the future, okay?"

"I'll do my damnedest."

I had Janine wait on the outside balcony while I swept the room for threats. Everything seemed untouched, including the snack food and liquor on the sideboard. After returning my firearm to my waistband, I helped myself to a handful of salt-and-pepper potato chips from an open bag, followed by a single-serving packet of gummy fish. Nothing like a quick dose of carbohydrates, salt and sugar to fend off exhaustion for another few minutes.

"Frankie's pacing the sidewalk," Janine said, entering the room.

"Yeah, she's really wound up. I can't blame her."

"It's passive-aggressive."

"What would you prefer? She starts firing her gun in the air?" I unzipped my duffel bag, fished out my underarm deodorant, and generously swiped my armpits. For good measure, I slipped the stick down my pants and gave my taint a pine-scented once-over. Although my intentions were good—my funk was powerful—Janine grimaced as if I'd popped a bag of cow poop over our stuff.

"Are you serious?" Janine stuffed her clothes into her bag. "You know the aluminum in that deodorant gives you cancer, right?"

"I do. And you know how I know that?"

"Because I've told you a thousand times to stop using it on your crotch?"

"Doesn't damage the equipment." I winked at her. "Want a quickie? Frankie can wait."

"Are you kidding?"

"Yeah, I am. But you're cute when you're angry."

Struggling to not smile, she hurled a rolled-up pair of socks at my head. As I ducked, I wondered yet again how she was processing her killing that man in the woods, the Nazi cowboy with the six-shooter who almost murdered us all before she finished him with a well-timed shotgun blast. She seemed fine, but these things had a way of boiling beneath the surface, sometimes for years. The nightmares would come. In the meantime, I took cold comfort in how well she held herself together.

"We got to work on your aim," I said, jamming the socks into my duffel along with the rest of my stuff. "Let's get outside before Frankie blows a gasket, or the clerk downstairs calls the cops."

After one last sweep to make sure we had all of our gear, I hoisted our bags and led Janine out of the room. Frankie had taken a position behind the low brick wall that separated the hotel's courtyard from the street, her pistol pressed against her hip.

"Everything okay?" I asked as we approached.

"Fine," she said. "I got a little paranoid about a car, but it's leaving."

"Which one?"

Frankie jutted her chin to our left, where a pair of brake lights flared before disappearing around a corner. "Probably nothing, but it paused across the street a little too long."

"At this point, I don't worry until they start shooting," I said, hefting the bags. "We're ready."

"Janine, let's get to the van." Frankie stepped onto the sidewalk, her head darting in every direction. "Jake, you'll follow in your truck?"

"At some point, we're going to need to go by our house," I said.

"No, you don't." Frankie rolled her eyes. "It's too dangerous, remember? Unknown unknowns?"

"I'll recon, slip in. You know I can do it." I walked toward my truck. "There's cash at our place, passports, some other stuff we'll need. Tell me the address of the safe house."

"It's not on a street."

"Then give me the coordinates, sis. I know what I'm doing." Unlocking the truck, I opened the driver's door and pulled the hood release.

"Our passports are upstairs," Janine said. With her arms crossed over her chest, she rubbed her elbows in tight, fast circles. "Spare cash in the bear."

Walking to the front of the vehicle, I opened the hood and peered into the engine for anything amiss. "I once had to drive through Fallujah in the middle of a riot. Now that was a bad idea. Driving to my house, it's just a kinda-poor idea, you know what I mean?"

"If you're that worried about car bombs, I'll pay that clerk inside five bucks to start your car," Frankie said.

"Nah, he was a nice guy. He gave me a mint when we checked out." Praying for a street clear of witnesses for another few minutes, I eased myself onto the pavement and scooted beneath the truck, running my hands along the undercarriage. Too late, I remembered the flashlight I always kept in the glove compartment, but nothing on the frame felt out of place.

"No bombs," I said, once I crawled free of the vehicle and stood, wiping my hands on my pants. "See you at the safe house, okay? Text me those coordinates." I flicked up my shirt, giving Frankie a view of the pistol in my waistband. Not that it would ease her worrying.

Frankie sighed. "Oh, bullshit. I'm going with you."

I smirked. "Knew you would."

7

Late at night, with little traffic, it took Frankie and me fifty minutes to drive from the hotel to my home on the Snake River. The Monkey Man was escorting Janine to the safe house, and as much as I hated to leave her, it was for the best. This was a stealth mission. Ninjas only.

Once we left I-84 for US-26, and the road narrowed to two lanes, we only encountered one other vehicle: a massive truck that whipped past outside of the flyspeck of Notus, scattering onions in its wake. Onion-harvesting season had an early start this year, maybe because of the intense heat.

Frankie had her phone out, flicking through a few days' worth of emails and text messages. "You get that wedding invite from Andrew? I guess he's getting hitched in New Orleans."

I chuckled. "Yeah. You thinking of going?"

"Maybe. Haven't seen him in years. Thought he was pissed at me."

"You give him reason to get pissed off?"

"Maybe? Last time I saw him, it was at a house party. And I told a joke."

"Uh-oh."

"I said: 'What's a dyslexic's favorite sex position?'"

"You knew he was dyslexic, right?"

"Sure, but I temporarily forgot, probably because I was drinking hard. Nobody said anything, so I yelled the punchline:

'Ninety-six! They rub their backs together!' Then Andrew yelled, 'I'm dyslexic, you bitch!'" She shrugged. "Nobody's got a sense of humor anymore."

"You should go."

"I'll need to load up on more jokes. You're not going?"

"Even if we weren't neck-deep in some spectacular shit, no. I got too much going on." And not enough money to take the family to a wedding in New Orleans, I didn't add.

"You're always busy, bro. You need to relax."

"I got a mortgage. Besides, I relax."

"Liar."

"What do you call fishing? And drinking too much beer?"

"Fine, point taken. Well, I might go. Always liked Andy." She slipped her phone back in her pocket.

We passed through Parma, and I spared a glance at the Quik-Stop gas station on the main road. A lone clerk sat behind the register, his head bent to a phone. A few nights ago, Ted Baker's friends had gunned down everyone inside, one of the many events that eventually drew my family into the woods. No doubt some unlucky employee had mopped up the blood and repaired the bullet holes in the walls, erasing all signs of massacre so the great wheels of commerce could roll on.

Two miles past the Quik-Stop, we took a left, rumbling over the railroad tracks and past the seedy box of the local strip club, its parking lot filled with trucks. This was the edge of town, the line of true darkness. "Think anyone's up there?" Frankie asked.

"At the house?" I said. "No, but better safe than sorry. Hope you're ready to get muddy, sis."

I flicked my headlights onto the lowest setting. At the next intersection, rather than take a left onto the road that ran past our house, I bumped onto the dirt track that ran parallel to it through the hop fields. The massive wooden frames that farmers erected to support the hop bines, threaded with webs of rough string, would screen the truck from the road and anyone on our property. Turning the headlights off, I let the truck rumble forward at walking pace, crunching over fallen leaves and dry soil. When I estimated that I had overshot the house, I braked and shut down the engine.

"What's the play?" Frankie whispered.

"We watch."

Exiting the truck, we stepped carefully over furrows, hands outstretched against any taut strings or wooden poles in our path. The pale flank of my house flickered into view. I crouched beside a trellis, knowing already that something was wrong. My side yard featured all the usual debris, including a sawhorse bench, an all-weather tool chest, and my fishing boat beneath its white cover. But the faint moonlight also glinted off a bit of chrome tucked behind the boat—the rear bumper of a car that didn't belong to me. It wouldn't have been visible from the road until I turned into my driveway, too late to save me from who-ever was waiting.

"Company," I whispered to Frankie. "Give me your phone."

She handed it over, and I clicked it on, cupping my hand to block the light from the screen. "What's your passcode?"

"Zero-six-six-six."

"Imaginative." I typed it in, and the phone unlocked. Frankie had selected a photograph of a gold-plated AK-47 as her home-screen wallpaper.

"Bite me." Frankie snorted. "I bet yours is one-two-three-four or some easy crap."

"No comment." I dialed my house line.

As much as I hated the idea of having a landline in the house, Janine had insisted we install one. Cell reception isn't always the greatest around here, she told me again and again. What if we had an emergency and our mobile phones didn't work?

The way I figured it, the landline was another thirty dollars per month up in smoke. But when you're married, you make com-promises, and in exchange for putting up with Janine's paranoia about cell reception, she gave me a little peace about my ever-expanding gun collection. As I raised Frankie's phone to my ear, though, I was glad that Janine had pushed the issue.

The house phone rang seven, eight, nine times before the answering machine clicked to life. My own voice invited me to leave a message, followed by the beep. "Hey, sweetie," I said, cupping a hand over my mouth. "I'm running a little late. Bit of an accident in Parma. Should be there in fifteen. Love ya."

I hung up and settled back on my haunches, my ears straining for any sounds below the click and hum of insects. A thump from within the house, and the kitchen window lit. The back door creaked open, and a man appeared on the edge of the porch, a flashlight snapping to life in his hand. He was middle-aged, his colossal head shaved, his every feature blocky and sharp.

I lay flat in the dirt, Frankie tucking next to me, in case the man flicked his light in our direction. Instead, he focused the beam on the yard, where another hulk of a man sat in the grass.

"Bruce," the man with the flashlight hissed. "He's on his way. Best get that ass in gear."

Bruce sighed and stood, his knees cracking, and drew a pistol from a holster on his belt. Like the man on the porch, he was older, his thinning gray hair swept tightly against his skull, his blue polo shirt and faded jeans barely holding back his swelling gut.

"Get in position," the first man said, waving the flashlight toward my boat.

"Which direction he coming from?"

"From Parma, which means you're on this side of the boat. Got it?"

Grunting, Bruce lumbered to my boat and crouched on the starboard side. The light bolted to the roof of the house, usually triggered by the motion detector angled toward the driveway, stayed dark. They must have disabled it, thinking the night gave them an advantage, but two could play at that game.

The man on the porch retreated inside, and the kitchen light clicked off. I could see a handful of mistakes in the ambush they had set up, but I still debated whether we should retreat. Charging into yet another building filled with enemy combatants struck me as tempting fate, especially after the bloodshed at that creepy clubhouse. That said, capturing at least one of these guys alive seemed like our best chance at finding out who else might want us dead.

"Go north," I whispered to my sister. "Anyone on the perimeter, take them out."

"What are you going to do?"

"Clear."

She shook her head. "By yourself?"

"I have a plan. I'm keeping your phone."

"Okay, cowboy macho asshole."

"Thanks for your support." Clapping her on the back, I stood and crept through the fields until I was well south of my property, then crossed the road, staying low. This far out in the country, nobody bothered to install roadway lighting, which meant I was relying on my internal map more than my eyesight. Turning back toward my house, I walked on the shoulder until my boots splashed mud. I had reached the shallow irrigation ditch that ran along the edge of my driveway.

I crouched, orienting myself. On the far side of the driveway, a lone pine would shield some of my approach, but it was still twenty-five feet or so to the boat—over gravel and dry twigs. I needed a distraction.

Unlocking Frankie's phone, I dimmed the screen before swiping through apps, praying she had installed the streaming-music one I needed. Hiding in the dark a few feet from a gunman is an awkward time to wait for something to download. Fortunately, she had the right app. I tapped it open, logged Frankie out, and inputted my own username and password.

My playlists appeared, loaded with the classic heavy metal that I used to stay awake during long commutes. Motörhead was perfect for this occasion. I tapped the little icon on the bottom of the screen that allowed me to select my device, then chose the web-enabled stereo in my living room.

As I tapped the appropriate song ("Ace of Spades") and thumbed up the volume, I remembered how Janine and I had argued over that stereo. How I insisted that I didn't need yet another device connected to the web, even if it was the same price as the alternatives. I lost that battle, but now I was glad she talked me into it.

Guitars shrieked out the house's dark windows, followed by Lemmy Kilmister wailing about gambling and luck. I stood, slipping around the pine, phone back in my pocket and the 9mm in my right hand. I passed the big black car these men had arrived in, a brand-new Mercedes with Idaho plates.

As I hoped, Bruce had turned instinctively to face the music pumping from the house, his gun limp in his hand. From five feet away, I heard him mutter a question to himself. Then I had him. I drove my arm straight, plowing the pistol-barrel into his jaw as his head turned. The impact sent him back a step, his gun rising until I grabbed his wrist, slotted my right foot behind his left one, and pushed him onto the ground. Lemmy howled for the heavens as I drove a foot into the side of Bruce's face once, twice, three times, knocking him cold.

No windows in my living room faced onto the driveway, so I felt safe enough to stuff my 9mm in my waistband and open the tool chest beside the boat. Working by feel, I retrieved a roll of duct tape, a screwdriver, and a couple lengths of nylon rope. Kneeling beside Bruce, I taped his mouth and bound his hands and feet, finishing the last knot as the music cut out. Someone inside the house cursed loudly.

Gripping Bruce by the ankles, I dragged him into the shadow of the boat before rooting through his pockets. I found a wallet and phone, which I pocketed, along with a spare clip for his weapon.

I paused to take a breath, my shirt damp with sweat, my lungs burning. That little fight had burned more energy than I expected. I was running on fumes.

After popping out its magazine, I slipped Bruce's pistol beneath the boat cover. Not the best hiding place, but it would take the weapon out of play until I could clear the house. Crouching beside Bruce, I listened for doors opening, footsteps on the porch, anything to indicate that someone was coming outside. I could try to draw them out one at a time, but I suspected these guys were too smart for that.

A window slid open. "Bruce," someone hissed. "You out there?"

The voice was coming from the small bathroom window that overlooked the driveway. Whoever was in there could only see darkness, otherwise they would have raised some kind of alarm. I expected them to turn on a light, but nothing happened.

"Bruce?"

I grunted.

"False alarm on the music," the voice said. "You okay?"

I grunted again.

"We got like five minutes. I'm gonna take a dump."

"Now?" Someone else shouted from deeper in the house. "Taking a shit now?"

So I was dealing with at least two other guys. Good to know. Standing as quietly as I could, I moved toward the house, taking care to swing wide of the window.

"Yeah, man, when you gotta go, you gotta go." The clunk of a toilet seat lowering. "And don't worry, I'm leaving the window open. I'll even light a match for you, sweetheart."

"Don't turn on the light," the other voice said. "Don't wanna ruin our operational leverage."

Pressing myself against the side of the house, I crept toward the bathroom window, thankful that I had planted grass along this side of the driveway last summer. Closing in, I pulled my phone out of my pocket, flicked it on, and activated the music app again.

Motörhead blasted out the window. Deep in the house, that other man screamed in confusion and rage. The man on the toilet cursed. I was close enough to hear him slapping at the toilet-paper holder, trying to clean up before he stood.

I pushed my upper body through the window. The toilet was to the immediate right, and the man sitting on it only had time to turn his head before I had him around the neck, dragging him into the night. His hands gripped my forearms and pulled, strong, but I braced my feet against the side of the house and used that leverage to jerk his body over the sill.

We landed in the driveway with him on top of me, hard enough to drive the air out of my lungs. I wrapped my legs around his torso, pinning him in place as I slid my forearm around his neck, elbow beneath his chin, and squeezed. With my other hand against the back of his head, pushing him into the choke, it only took a few seconds for him to pass out.

The music cut out again. "Damnit," yelled the man in my living room.

I had to work quickly now. Dragging my latest victim to the boat, I taped his mouth and bound his hands and feet, leaving his pants down around his ankles. Bruce was beginning to stir, so I knelt and punched him in the head again. I was beyond caring whether I was doing permanent damage. At least I was letting them live for the moment.

The man from the bathroom had no weapons on him aside from a pocketknife. He must have left his gun inside the house. A loose weapon made things a bit more problematic.

"Dwayne," called the man inside. "Where the hell are you?" As I pressed against the side of the house again—all this back-and-forth was getting exhausting—footsteps stormed down my hallway. He was approaching the bathroom.

I drew my 9mm and aimed it at the empty window.

"Dwayne? You there?"

The bathroom light clicked on, revealing a windowsill cracked from when I dragged Dwayne over it. The man noticed the damage. A gasp, followed by cloth rustling, and a click. I tensed. A pistol barrel poked out the window, followed by the silhouette of a head.

Darting forward, I slapped my hand over the man's hands on the pistol and smashed them against the sill. The weapon tumbled away, the man yelping in fear and surprise. I already had my own firearm dug into his temple, my finger on the trigger.

In the bathroom light, I finally had a good look at a familiar face.

"Jim," I said. "How goes it?"

"Fine, Jake." Jim's face poured sweat.

I grinned. "Well, this is awkward."

8

After I left the military, I found myself at loose ends, feeling weaker and more useless with every passing week.

And then the Cab of the Future came into my life.

Boise is not a cab kind of town. People own their own cars or motorcycles. Pour a couple drinks in them, and they might shell out forty or fifty bucks for a cab, but just as often they climb behind the wheel of their vehicle and tempt fate. I've known my share of people who decided that five shots of whiskey had turned them into a champion driver at the Indy 500, only to end up splattered like a bug across their crumpled dashboard.

A couple of years back, a not-so-brilliant dude with the brilliant name of Hanzo Sandman decided to introduce Boise to the Cab of the Future, a Nissan minivan with USB charging ports, a giant sunroof, extra legroom for passengers, and rugs woven from a fiber that wipes out odors. Sandman, who wanted the city to sign a contract with him for fifty of the vehicles, decided to gin up some publicity by dressing up like an old-fashioned driver, complete with a cap and white gloves, and motoring passengers wherever their hearts desired. On his third trip, on a desolate downtown corner, he picked up Stevie "Big" Johnson.

Stevie and I had gone to the same high school, only he dropped out in ninth grade. Considering the number of concussions he dealt out, the state was probably relieved to see him go. Stevie had followed up his illustrious school career by founding an internet company that he sold within a few years, making him a billion-aire. I'm kidding. Actually, Stevie inhaled meth until his teeth fell out. He made money by robbing the occasional liquor store, along with petty theft.

When Sandman tooted up in the Cab of the Future, smiling and eager to please, Stevie must have regarded that yellow hunk of crap as a gift from whatever dark demon he worshipped. I wonder to this day if Sandman considered hitting the gas when Stevie flashed him a toothless smile. Whatever thoughts of escape might have gone through Sandman's head, they did him no good when Stevie climbed into the front passenger seat, bypassing the thick partition between the front and back areas, and placed a dinky pistol against Sandman's temple.

Stevie needed a ride. He had a game plan that day, his own meth-fueled version of starting an internet firm.

Meanwhile I was in a bar near downtown, chugging beers like no tomorrow. I had a bit of an issue back then, in the year after I left the military. The bar was a new hipster joint where every beer on tap came from a microbrewery with a poetic name, and every item on the menu was organic and grass-fed. Any leftovers from your meal ended up in a compost pile in the base-ment. I cared about none of that. I wanted a dark box where I could drink myself into oblivion while staring at a baseball game, and the bartender, a decent guy with a handlebar moustache named Sam Bean, only bothered me once an hour or so.

"What you do for a living, mister?" he asked at one point.

He might have wanted me out of there before I did something impolite, like vomit on the floor. "I'm a professional drinker," I said, saluting him with my half-empty glass. "Preparing for the Olympics. Working on my endurance." I pointed at his suit and tie and asked: "Why you wearing that? You look like you got a job interview."

He shrugged. "Dress for the job you want, not the job you have."

"How long you been a bartender?"

He offered me a dead stare. "About twelve years." After that, our interactions consisted of him wordlessly refilling my beer whenever I raised my empty glass.

When Stevie walked through the front doors, I recognized trouble. Mostly because he entered with that stupid little firearm pointed at Sam Bean's funky facial hair. I was too drunk to feel anything but a vague annoyance at my afternoon being interrupted. A stickup meant cops, and the cops would make mean comments about my presence in a drinking establishment in the middle of a workday. I placed my hands on the bar, fingers spread wide, and waited for Stevie's next move.

Although Stevie had sat three desks away from me for years, I didn't recognize him. This might come as a shock, but years of drugs have a funny way of transforming stocky blonde children into creatures who look like skeletons with cheap skin stretched across the bones.

"Gim munny," Stevie announced.

Sam Bean squinted. "I'm sorry, what?"

"Munny gimme it," Stevie muttered.

Through the bar's front windows, the Cab of the Future idled at the curb, Sandman at the wheel. He caught my eye and offered a sympathetic shrug, as if to say: *see what I do for customers?* It turned out later that Sandman had some pretty big mental issues, including a pathological need to please. Histrionic personality disorder, it's called.

"What?" Sam Bean said again. "I want to help, but I can't understand you."

"Munny," Stevie enunciated carefully, tongue lolling from his mouth, pistol wavering. "Wanna munny."

I shook myself from my alcoholic stupor in time to realize I had come to the bar with my pistol in a concealed-carry holster under my shirt, because that was the most responsible way to go drinking. I have no excuses for my behavior in those days, but go ahead and throw the first stone.

In the bar's tastefully recessed lighting, Stevie's skin reddened, his tongue flapping a little faster as his blood boiled. In a couple of seconds, something very bad was going to happen here, all because Sam Bean couldn't interpret Meth Space Alien.

I drew my pistol. Maybe not the smartest move, but what choice did any of us have? Even with my blood alcohol level so high my piss was probably flammable, I had pretty good aim. My bullet only missed him by five feet, smashing some pricey specialty glasses on a shelf along the wall.

Stevie spun on me.

Oh shit, I thought, I'm dead.

"Why doin' that, man?" Stevie said. "Why you no love me?"

Now it was my turn to cock a weird eyebrow, mirroring Sam Bean's earlier expression. I fired again, aiming for Stevie's center mass, but the bullet only chewed away a chunk of nearby table. Dammit.

Stevie, deciding that a gunfight wasn't in his best interest, turned and ran out of the bar. I should have placed my gun on the table and thanked whatever saint watches over drunks that he hadn't decided to fire back at me. Instead I stood and headed for the front door, tall as a cowboy in an old Western movie. Maybe a part of me was thinking of my daddy the lawman, fighting for righteousness. Or maybe a part of me hungered to deliver some old-fashioned hurt.

I marched outside the bar as Stevie dove into the front passenger seat of the Cab of the Future. Through the tinted rear window I saw Sandman, eager to please, rise out of his seat as he stood on the gas pedal. The minivan rolled down the street, slowly gaining speed. I had all the time in the world to pause on the sidewalk and line up my shot.

My four bullets went into the front tire and engine block as the Cab of the Future squealed into a turn at the end of the block. The tire exploded with a bang louder than my gunshots, and the minivan fishtailed to a stop so sudden it sent Stevie—who must have forgotten to buckle his seatbelt—through the windshield neat as you please. By the time I made the corner, he was on his feet in the middle of the intersection, bloody and flailing his arms and screaming but still alive, at least for the next three seconds.

Sandman stomped on the gas and the Cab of the Future leapt forward, spraying orange sparks from its wrecked front rim. I suspect he only wanted to escape, but Stevie leapt in front of the charging vehicle and raised his pistol. Two tons of metal smashed him flat.

Behind me, Sam Bean, who had come out of the bar to witness the commotion, vomited on his polished shoes. Down the street, a kid with a smartphone captured the whole scene in high definition, posting it to the web before I could holster my gun.

The first cop on the scene was Jim, then a grizzled twenty-year man, who took one look at the carnage, offered me a hearty handshake, and said: "Thank you for taking that little prick out of the gene pool." For him, this was another boring Tuesday.

By the end of the week, the kid's forty-second video clip had attracted two million eyeballs on YouTube, and I had a phone call from Janine at The Bond King, wondering whether I wanted a job as a bounty hunter.

"Aren't you afraid I'm a loose cannon?" I asked.

"Naw," she said. "Better a loose cannon than a dead one, you know what I mean?"

That made zero sense, but I took the gig. If nothing else, it was a chance to put a little order back in the world. With much sweating and white-knuckling, I also quit drinking so much. I felt a little bad about Stevie, although I could tell myself that he never contributed much to the world anyway, aside from deep-sixing any chance of those stupid cabs cruising the streets of Boise.

During my early career as a bounty hunter, I called Jim often. As much as cops make a big show of disdaining bounty hunters, they're willing to share information with our kind when it's useful to them, and I always tried to be as useful as possible to him. I even thought we developed a friendship of sorts, at least until he showed up at my house one night with a group of armed men.

9

"You're going to place your hands on the sill," I told Jim. "Then you're going to very smoothly climb out the window to me. Understand?"

Jim nodded.

"Is there anyone else in the house?"

"One more. My client. She's unarmed, okay?"

"Client?"

"Someone who wants to speak to you." Jim squinted into the night. "You didn't kill my boys, did you?"

"They're tied up. Nothing harmed but their dignity." Keeping the pistol against his temple, I lashed out with my right foot, sending his dropped weapon into the dark. "Come on."

Grunting, Jim swung a leg over the sill and climbed into the driveway, taking his time. It was odd to see him out of uniform. For tonight's excursion, he had opted for a stylish pair of faded jeans and a long-sleeved gray shirt stained with oil. His police belt had an empty holster on his right hip, a stubby walkie-talkie clipped to the left. His feet plopped onto the gravel, and he paused to take a shuddering breath. "I need to retire," he said, trying out a small smile.

"I don't care."

The smile faded. "Get that gun out of my face."

"Let's go back inside, you first." I dug the barrel into his skull, making sure he felt it. "This goes wrong, you die first.

Keep that in mind."

We marched around the driveway to the rear of the house, ascending the porch. The light snapped on, illuminating my big cooler beside the table where my family ate dinner whenever it was warm. Usually I kept that red monstrosity loaded with ice and beer so I could pop open a can or two before I went into the house after a long shift, but as we walked past, I noted it was open—and empty except for a gallon of meltwater. The bastards had guzzled down all my alcohol while they waited for me to show up. No wonder I had taken them all down without much of an issue.

Jim pushed the back door open, and I gripped the back of his neck before he could step into the darkness of the kitchen. Grinding my pistol between his shoulder blades, I shoved him forward, ducking a bit to hide my profile behind his bulk. The first floor of our house was an open design, with only a waist-high divider between the kitchen and the living room, which turned it into a kill-box for anyone firing from the stairwell that led to the second floor. At least if someone took a shot, it would hit Jim first.

"Please," Jim said, his voice high and reedy. "Would you turn the light on? Jake is behind me."

I took the initiative, using my elbow to slap the switches on the panel beside the door. The overhead light in the living room clicked on, revealing a middle-aged woman at the table, an open can of beer in front of her. She wore an expensive pantsuit, a white dress shirt open at the collar, and pearls. She was blonde, her face deeply lined, and you might have mistaken her for any woman in an upscale boutique until you saw her eyes, which were green and steely in a way that reminded me of snipers I knew during the war.

"Jake," she said, and smiled, waving for me to sit across from her.

"I'm fine right here, thanks," I said, keeping Jim in front of me as I sidestepped in front of the fridge. From here, I had a good view of her hands on the table, along with the stairwell.

The lady frowned. "Suit yourself. I'm Karen."

"Funny," I said. "You don't look much like a goddess."

Karen cocked her head. "I'm not quite sure how to take that."

"Never mind. Something Keith said."

Karen's eyebrows lifted. "Keith Baker? Where is he?"

"He's safe. Don't you worry about that."

"That's good," Karen said. "That's very important, that he's safe. He's a former cop, you know. You hurt him, and I think some of his former colleagues will be very upset."

"And how do you know him?"

"He's my nephew. I'm Ted Baker's sister."

"He didn't mention you."

"Ted? I don't imagine so. We were pretty estranged. You know what that means?"

I snorted. "You take a tour of the house? You notice that library upstairs?"

"So I'm not dealing with an idiot. That's good, too. It'll make things easier."

"What do you want?"

Before she could reply, a gunshot echoed through the night. I ducked, my finger tensing on the trigger, but no windows cracked. In my grip, Jim whined and shook. Karen startled a bit before settling back, as if home invasion and pistol fire were everyday parts of her life. She snapped at Jim: "What was that?"

"Don't know, ma'am," Jim mumbled.

The shot had come from north of the house. "You lied to me," I told him, tightening my hand on his neck until I felt his arteries throbbing. "How many more you got out there?"

Jim took a deep breath. "One on the perimeter, two hundred yards up. He was supposed to stay up there, radio if he saw cars."

I glanced through the kitchen window. No headlights, nothing out of the ordinary.

The walkie-talkie on Jim's belt crackled. "Bro?" Frankie asked.

"Hand it back," I told Jim. "Slow."

He obeyed orders, and I removed my hand from his neck so I could take the walkie-talkie. Pushing the button to talk, I said: "Sis?"

Frankie chuckled. "You get the rest of them?"

"I think so."

"Did you kill that man?" Jim asked, almost yelling, his neck flushing red.

"Who is that?" Frankie asked.

"You remember Jim MacLeod? Cop from Boise?"

"Oh yeah, dumb as a post." Frankie laughed again. "Jim, your friend was on my brother's property with a gun. I had no choice. Self-defense."

"Is he dead?" Jim yelled.

Frankie sighed. "I'm coming up, bro. Don't shoot me."

"Come through the back," I said. "You alone?"

"Yeah."

Without shifting my eyes from Karen, I set the walkie-talkie on the counter to my left. "All those guys you brought," I asked Jim. "They cops?"

"They're all good men," Jim said, his voice wavering. "I know we're on your property, but we just wanted to talk, I swear."

"You were waiting in the dark, with guns. I could have killed them all, and any jury in the state would have let me walk. You know how it goes out here."

"I'm not sure you're accurate on your legalities there," Karen raised her hands, palms up, as if weighing two invisible lumps. "It's manslaughter, potentially, depending on circumstances."

"How would you know?" I asked.

"Let's say I spent a little time in law school."

"Good for you." As footsteps echoed on my porch, I shifted my body slightly so that Jim was angled between me and whoever walked through the back door. I was ninety-nine percent sure it was my sister, but it's always that one-percent uncertainty that gets you killed.

The footsteps stopped to the left of the door. "Bro?"

"In here," I called. "It's clear."

The door creaked, and Frankie appeared, her UMP pointed at Karen. "I know you," Frankie said.

Karen smiled. "And I know you, my dear."

"Is he dead?" Jim almost shouted.

"Calm down. That gunshot was his. I knocked him out." Not slowing down, Frankie swung into the living room, keeping a wall behind her at all times as she squinted at Karen. "You're a federal prosecutor or something, aren't you?"

"Or something," Karen said.

"If my memory serves, you sent George Lincoln up for twelve years, right, on weapons charges?"

Karen nodded. "And I've put away a lot of bad men like him, Francesca. I know a lot about you, too."

"Everyone calls me 'Frankie,'" Frankie said through gritted teeth.

"Oh. I do apologize." The edges of Karen's mouth twitched as she struggled not to smile. "I don't recall reading 'Frankie' in your file."

"Really." Frankie's hand flexed on her UMP's grip. "That file, did it mention any nicknames?"

"I believe one of your *alleged* acquaintances referred to you repeatedly as a 'Blue Steel Bitch.'"

"I kind of like that," I said. "It's cool."

"Shut up," Frankie snarled, positioning herself directly behind Karen. "So why don't you tell us why you're here. You got a warrant?"

"She's Ted Baker's sister," I said.

"So this is revenge." Frankie raised the rifle. "Bad idea."

Karen chuckled, as if she were dining on steaks with a group of rich folks instead of sitting in a living room with a gun pointed at the back of her head. "I didn't like my brother very much. A number of years back, I tried hosting a fundraiser for Hillary, when she ran for president?" She sighed. "I plead temporary insanity, trying to do something like that in Idaho. Anyway, Ted shows up, grabs the microphone, and calls everyone in the room a 'cuck,' whatever that means, along with a bunch of other unmentionables."

"I take it Ted was a Trump supporter?" I asked.

"He liked a lot of what Trump was selling, but ultimately Ted didn't care too much about politics. He made his money, he did horrible things with it, and then one day you killed him."

"We don't know anything about murdering him," I said.

"I got a lot of Ted's files. They automatically uploaded to the cloud, probably from his laptop and phone, and I have his passwords. Not that he knew that, or he would have denied me access. I know he forced you to participate in that terrible game. He wouldn't have let you come out of those woods alive, not while he was still living."

"You got the evidence, arrest us," Frankie said. "Otherwise, screw off."

"I'm not a prosecutor anymore. I enjoyed doing it, and we did a lot of good for the state, but I decided to call it quits. Now I'm a private attorney, although now that you wiped out my brother, I guess I'm also taking over his fried-chicken empire, aren't I?"

"If you're taking that role," I said, "can I make a suggestion? The chicken sandwich they sell, it's got too much tomato and lettuce on it. I don't want half a salad to get in the way of clogging up my arteries, you know?"

Jim snorted laughter.

Karen's mouth tightened into a bloodless line. "I will take that under advisement."

"Thanks. Big help." I was feeling a little better, more in control, even with exhaustion making my reflexes sludgy. "You know what else would be a big help? Telling us why you're here."

Karen took a sip of beer, wincing. "Not my usual brand," she said, pushing the can aside with a finger. "In addition to my brother, I'm assuming you killed a lot of other folks with money and connections. Which means that, unless some kind of miracle presents itself, you're dead. Am I right?"

"We're still breathing," Frankie said.

Karen smirked. "You have a big pair of balls for a lady, Francesca. I'll give you that. But balls aren't enough. Either they shoot you down in the street, or you're killed in jail. I'm here to deliver the miracle of life."

"We're all ears," I said.

"I have a job for you. If you complete it, I'll make sure that every trace of this situation is buried so deep that nobody will ever find it, and you have my word on that." Karen shifted in her seat so she could look over her shoulder at Frankie. "Now, I expect your next statement will be, 'We can't take you at your word.' I'm telling you, dear, you don't have a choice."

"What's the job?" Frankie said.

Karen pointed at Jim. "He needs to go outside. He can't hear this."

If I released Jim, he would free his men beside the boat, who might decide to do something stupid. My instincts told me not to take that chance.

"They won't try to come in here," Karen said, reading my thoughts. "Right, Jim?"

"Where's my man you hit?" Jim asked Frankie.

"On the lawn, right by the fence," Frankie said. "I cuffed him."

"I appreciate you not killing him."

"Whatever."

I shoved Jim forward. He stumbled, recovered, and then, rubbing his neck, disappeared through the back door, never looking back. Once he left, I closed the door and locked it.

"So what's the job?" Frankie asked, lowering the UMP a few inches.

"It's unpleasant, I'm warning you now." Karen's eyes flicked away. "There's someone in my life who needs to go away."

"You're going to need to give us more than that," Frankie said.

"Not at the moment," Karen said, her gaze darting around my living room. After my little stunt with the stereo, maybe she was paranoid of my electronics. I guessed it was possible to set any kind of internet-enabled device to listen and record a conversation, although I had never seen it done.

"Lady, I might have done some bad crap in my life," Frankie said, "but we're not hired killers. Whoever's bothering you, maybe we could talk to them. Break a leg or an arm, if it came to that."

"That's if whatever they did to you rises to the level of arm-breaking," I added cheerfully. "I mean, maybe we can just give them a good noogie."

Karen's eyebrows twitched in confusion. "A noogie?"

"God, weren't you ever in elementary school?" I mimed putting someone in a headlock, then rubbing my knuckles hard against their scalp. "A noogie. Hurts like hell. Whatever this person is doing to you, they'll never do it again. I guarantee it."

Karen no longer looked confused; if anything, she seemed pained. Well, my sense of humor is an acquired taste.

"My brother's jokes aside," Frankie said, "we're not professional killers."

"I'm sorry, but you're criminals." Karen offered a polite little laugh, as if someone had made a *faux pas* at a cocktail party. "Don't give me that usual line about how you have a code of honor, or how you're not like other criminals, or how you only do something out of necessity. You're going to get this done, because you have no choice."

A vein ticked in Frankie's left temple. I raised a hand, but I was too far away to squeeze her arm, a gesture that might have broken the engine of rage cycling to life behind her eyes. Whatever the circumstances, trying to give my sister an order was an invitation to have her feed you into a woodchipper—headfirst, if you were lucky.

But Frankie only took a half step forward before she stopped, that vein ticking faster and faster. It was an astounding sight, like witnessing a skyscraper rocketing into the atmosphere. My sister, curbed for the first time in her life—because she knew, as I did, that we were in the presence of real power, the kind that could ultimately decide whether we lived or died.

"How are you getting this information to us?" Frankie asked in a tight, almost strangled voice.

Karen said, "If you give me an email address, I'll make sure you get what you need. As I said, it's going to be unpleasant— maybe more unpleasant than you realize right now. But you have my word that if you carry through, all this will go away."

Frankie recited a burner email I knew she used from time to time. "That it?"

"That's it." Karen stood to leave. "And don't worry, I'll make sure that those boys outside leave your property quietly. The last thing I want is someone putting a bullet in my Mercedes. I got it washed yesterday."

PART 2
WETWORK

10

After Karen and her busted-up bodyguards left, Frankie and I turned off all the lights and sat in the dark. Frankie positioned a chair so she could watch the road, while I opted to sit on the kitchen counter. I had no expectations of an ambush—not after Karen's brutal job offer—but one of her idiot henchmen might have returned for a little revenge, despite her assurances. As any bounty hunter will tell you, people will do stupid, borderline-suicidal things when they've been humiliated.

"Let them come," Frankie said, as if reading my thoughts. "We'll bury them near the river. Besides, those guys weren't killers."

"Nah, they were all cops or ex-cops. I knew that one guy."

"No wonder they were so easy to take. They were here to have a meeting with you, not kill you."

"I'm so tired of killing. At the rate we're racking up bodies, we're probably due for some kind of prize, right?" My voice rose into a decent imitation of an excitable game-show host: "Just shoot or blow up *four* more jackasses, and you'll win the *brand-new mountain bike.*"

"I wish this came with fabulous prizes." Frankie propped her chin in her hand. "You know what prize I want right now, more than anything? Twelve solid hours of sleep."

"Me, too."

"And a massage."

"I could go for one of those."

"I've been seeing a lot of that phrase pop up online, 'self-care'? Like, people deciding that their lives are so hard that they need to indulge on a regular basis, spas or 'sick days' or whatever. It's such a joke."

"People need to relax sometimes. You die otherwise."

"Sure, yeah, relax. I think I did that once. But 'self-care,' it's such an indulgent word, used by people who don't know what real pain is. Survive four years in Auschwitz, you're actually entitled to a little 'self-care.' Eat a whole chicken, down a bottle of scotch, shoot one of your former captors in the head, whatever you need to take the edge off."

"I really enjoy these weird little trips into your mind."

"Sorry, I'm tired. You think we can trust Karen?"

"Nope," I said. "And even if I did, if she wants a civilian killed, I'm not doing it. Self-defense is one thing, murder's another."

"Well, she figures she has us by the balls. And that's not the worst part. Once we kill this guy—assuming it's a guy—we've proven to Karen that we're willing to take orders. Then she's going to ask us to kill someone else, and then another person after that. As long as she knows what we did, the requests will never end."

"So she makes us her hired assassins."

"Sure. Here's something it took me a few years to realize: rich people have lawyers and fixers and maybe some bodyguards, but there are precious few hitmen out there. If Karen has a long kill list in her head, she might figure she's hit the jackpot with us."

"Her brother had men."

"Her brother was in bed with a bunch of very scary racists. I'm sure they did what he asked so long as he paid them. They were sledgehammers, not scalpels."

"We're not scalpels, or assassins, or anything like that."

"No, we are not, but that doesn't matter. She wants this done, and she's used to getting her way."

"How do we get out of this?"

"I don't know yet. This guy she wants us to kill, he might have something good on her, which is why we need to interrogate him rather than blasting a hole in him from two hundred yards."

Hopping off the counter, I opened the fridge and retrieved two cans of soda. "I'm sick of hurting people," I said, tossing one of the cans across the house.

Despite the darkness, Frankie caught the flying sugar-water easily. "I've definitely had my fill of hurting for the week. But I'm sicker of people threatening our family, so if we have to keep killing, so be it. I need to borrow one of your shovels."

11

Shovel in hand, Frankie walked out my back door and into the fields behind my house, muttering something under her breath as she did so. I followed at a distance, suspecting what was about to happen. If my hunch was correct, my sister had potentially put my family in danger.

Twenty yards beyond the crumbling shack at the edge of my property, our knees whispering in the thigh-high grass, Frankie stopped and turned, judging the angle from the dim blob of my house. "Yep, this is right." Driving the shovel into the dirt, she started digging, clumps of weedy dirt flying over her shoulder.

I stepped aside to dodge the debris. "Tell me you didn't."

"Relax, bro. It's beyond your fence. Nobody was going to come across it."

"I can't believe this. You know how pissed I am?"

"Based on your tone, really pissed? Don't worry, I buried it deep."

"Kids still come back here, Frankie."

"No guns in this one, okay? No ammo. So why don't you cut me a break?"

Her shovel smacked plastic. Tossing it aside, she stooped and cleared away more dirt with her hands, revealing a metal handle that she pulled. A bright orange bucket rose from the earth, its white lid dented by the shovel-edge. One of Frankie's caches. She buried these all over the state, loaded with everything she might need to survive on the run, but I had no idea she had planted one behind my house.

"Need a light?" I asked as she peeled the lid back.

"Nope." Reaching in, she pulled out a small flashlight and clicked it on. "I put one of these in every load, in case I have to dig it up at night."

The beam revealed a pair of phones, a stack of twenty-dollar bills in plastic wrap, a driver's license with Frankie's photo and the name "Susan P. Sanderson," a knife in a black plastic sheath, and a red metallic block with a cord wrapped around it. She plugged the cord into one of the phones, and its screen lit up.

"Long time ago," she said, "I had one of these buckets up near Rocky Canyon Hot Springs? I dig it up, and the phones were dead. They lose a charge after a couple months, even when off. From then on, I always throw one of these charger blocks into the bucket."

"That's so smart," I said, my voice bubbling with false cheer. "I can't believe you put a knife in there."

"Oh, come on, it's two feet down. No kids were going to dig it up." She offered me a middle finger before turning back to the phone. A new email in the inbox, sent from an address named, with an incredible amount of creativity, "JohnDoe1."

The email contained a name, "Anthony McKee," along with an address smack-dab in the middle of Boise. "Got it memorized?" Frankie asked.

"Sure."

"Okay." Frankie popped out the battery and SIM card, then dropped the phone between her feet and slammed the shovel onto it, cracking the screen. Another five blows reduced it to a mess of plastic and metal bits.

"Couldn't you use a VPN or something to check your email? Seems wasteful."

"You never know what new ways they have to track you," Frankie said, dumping the phone bits into her pocket. "That's why I'm still here, and many of my friends are not. Grab that knife, Mister Paranoid."

I did, and she tamped the lid onto the bucket before dropping it back into the hole. As she scooped the dirt back in, she winked at me. "For the record, I should have told you about this. I figured what you didn't know couldn't hurt you."

"Of course it could have hurt me. Why do people always use that phrase? There's zero truth in that phrase."

"I know, but it sounds so soothing." Twirling the shovel like a fighting staff, Frankie marched toward the house—only to stop and crouch as headlights slashed the darkness to our left. A black sedan turned into my driveway, followed by a police cruiser.

12

"Stay here," I told my sister, waving for her to duck.

"No, I'd totally walk up to the police with you," she muttered, sinking to her knees. "Just to say *howdy*."

The sedan braked at the head of my driveway and a hulk of a man climbed out, silhouetted by the cruiser headlights behind him: Harry, a homicide detective who had recently tried to upend my life. An unlit cigar jammed in his mouth, his hands sunk deep into the pockets of his off-the-rack slacks, he slouched toward my porch.

I'd spent my life around cops, and under normal circumstances I was relaxed around them. My years in the military had left me with no fear of authority, despite some top-notch screaming from various drill sergeants, lieutenants, and corporals. But these assembled cruisers made me afraid. What if they'd figured out what happened up north?

No, if we were suspects, they would have sent a SWAT team. This was something different.

Pausing before my front door, Harry bent his massive head to the tiny blue flame of a butane lighter, torching the tip of his cigar red.

I passed through the gap in the wire fence that marked the division between my yard and the back acreage, my hands visible at my sides. Startling a cop is an easy way to end up with a bullet in your gut, so I moved slowly and made as much noise as possible. "How's it going?" I called out.

Harry turned to me, blowing a smoke ring. "What are you doing, Jake?"

I threw my arms wide. "Hey, my property, remember?"

"You usually lurk around your property in the dead of night?"

"When I'm investigating weird noises, sure. You can't be too careful."

Harry looked beyond me, into the darkness that hid the river and the Oregon hills beyond. "What kind of weird noises?"

"Nothing. It was just a varmint. What can I do for you?"

"It's what we're doing for you, Jake. Bringing your guns back. That okay with you?"

After I found a dead girl in my gun safe, the cops took all of my weapons for testing. I had expected a drawn-out, bare-knuckle legal fight to get them back. "Sure," I said, somewhat stunned.

Harry nodded to one of the officers, who opened the trunk of the cruiser, revealing my guns wrapped in clear plastic. "Where you want them?" Harry asked.

"Porch is fine for now," I said. "I'll rack them up." I had no intention of letting any police into my house. I wondered if any of them noticed the damage to the bathroom window as they came up the driveway.

"No problem." Harry gestured, and the officers carried my weaponry to the edge of the porch. "Ordinarily, we'd make you come down to the station, retrieve your property, but I figured we'd do the neighborly thing, make a delivery."

"Because you need something."

"Well, 'need' is a strong term. But some information might be useful, if you have it."

"Where's your partner?" I asked, meaning Bob, a bony dude with the black, merciless eyes of a shark.

"He's on something else right now. Why, you miss him?"

"Absence makes the heart grow fonder. Anyway, what kind

of information you need?"

Harry closed in, his voice quieting: "Something very big happened up north. You have any idea what I'm talking about?"

"Your school actually won a football game?"

He laughed, smoke exploding from the corners of his mouth. "You can't be serious for a second, can you?"

"I'm always serious. You're not on my wavelength. But for your information, no, I haven't heard about anything happening 'up north.' Why don't you tell me?"

"Don't worry, you'll see it on the news in a day or two." He spoke at a near whisper. "Biggest thing to hit this state in years, maybe ever. Given your connections, I bet you'll hear something. Even if it's the finest bullshit, I want you to bring it to me, and only to me, understand?"

"Want the glory if it turns out to be something?"

"I'm a career-minded guy. No shame in that."

"What's in it for me?"

Harry jabbed his cigar at my porch, where the officers lined up the last of my rifles and pistols. "As you already know, none of those are the weapon that killed the girl in your house. You're free and clear."

"I'm so grateful. But you didn't answer my question."

"What do you want?"

"Lay off my sister."

"Come on, man. You know I can't do that."

"Sure, you can." I leaned closer, invading his airspace. "If this thing is big, and if I do something to help you crack it, you can absolutely lay off her."

"It's not my decision. A lot of cops want her put away. Heck, the FBI is interested, especially after that rocket-launcher shit I know she pulled."

"I get that. I'm not asking you to violate your duty. I'd want you to hunt her with a little less enthusiasm, if you get my meaning."

"We have a lot of open cases. Lot of them very important."

"Exactly."

"Okay. Oh, and one other thing." He tried to keep his tone casual. "You hear anything about an explosion at a warehouse over in Boise? Happened a couple hours ago?"

I shook my head. "I just been out here."

"Hunting varmints."

"That's right. Scaring them off."

"Well, okay then. You hear anything, you call, understand?"

"Sure do. Keep it stiff, detective."

Harry raised a pinky in the air. "Always do." With a final puff of noxious smoke, he turned away, trailing the cops as they piled into their cars. I stood at the end of my driveway and offered a final wave as they reversed into the road, leaving me in the insect-chattering dark. I took a deep breath and held it until my lungs burned.

13

After we loaded the weaponry into my gun safe, I retrieved the spare cash and passports, along with four books from atop Janine's extra-tall reading stack in the bedroom. If we had to hide out at the safe house for some time, she would appreciate the reading material. I returned to the kitchen to find Frankie standing in front of the open fridge, chugging the last of the orange juice.

"Take what you need," I told her. "We got to keep our strength up."

"I remember you telling me about the Army, they did that training where they kept you up for a week, right? No sleep, but you could eat whatever you wanted?" Tossing the orange juice container into the trash can, she retrieved the bottle of milk from the fridge's top shelf.

"Not an experience I want to relive," I said, depositing the books on the counter. The idea of raiding the food supplies seemed like a good one. I reached past Frankie and retrieved a hunk of mozzarella cheese from the bottom shelf, peeled back the wrapping, and wolfed it down.

As I chewed, Frankie checked out the spines of the books I'd brought downstairs.

"*Young Men and Fire*," she read aloud. "You ever get to that one?"

"No," I said. "I like Norman Maclean, though."

"It's pretty amazing." Raising a finger to pause the conversation, Frankie finished off the milk. Belched. "The book's about this forest fire, I think it was called the Mann Gulch Fire or something, killed a ton of smokejumpers after World War II. The part I remember is this one firefighter, the fire's rushing down on him, okay? And he does the craziest thing: he stops and sets a fire around him."

"Why would he do that?"

"Because the fire's rushing through grass. By setting his own fire, he deprives that bigger fire of fuel. He kneels down in the ashes, holds his breath, and the fire sweeps around him but doesn't touch him."

"Quick thinking."

"The book's full of stuff like that. All you ever wanted to know about fire science but were too scared to ask. Hey, and it changed how I burn down buildings."

"I love it when education enhances your life."

"So take that one, and the Stephen King one, and leave the other two. Hopefully we won't have to spend that much time hiding out."

From one of the kitchen cabinets I retrieved the boxes of animal crackers and cheese crackers that we usually kept for my daughter (sorry kid, I'll restock you the first chance I get) and escorted Frankie from the house. As I powered the truck down the roads leading back to the highway, my thoughts kept drifting to that fireman, whoever he was. You always think that you have grace and cool under pressure, then you hear a story like that, and it changes how you think about your own skills. If I were in a situation like that, confronted by a wall of fire, would I have the presence of mind to pull out my lighter and burn my way to safety?

I hoped so. I'd been in danger before, but that's the thing about danger: it can always escalate beyond your abilities. Over the past several days, I had found a dead girl in my gun safe, fought an Aryan Viking almost to the death, ended up in a police interrogation room—and all that was minor compared to running for my life through the hills of northern Idaho, chased by a bunch of rich bastards with far too many guns and zero qualms about skinning me alive.

The last time I felt this tired for so long had been in the desert, humping seventy pounds of gear through hundred-degree heat, always expecting that sniper shot to blow my redneck brains out the back of my skull. Now I was home, but the danger was still constant. A human being isn't built to withstand non-stop stress.

"About your gun safe," Frankie said, interrupting my thoughts as I bumped the truck onto the onramp to I-84.

"Uh-oh."

"You desperately need some upgrades. You should let me help you out. I get good discounts—one free Kalashnikov if I order a dozen, stuff like that."

"I only got two hands," I said, nodding toward the back seat, where a blanket covered my Beretta 12-gauge, the one weapon I'd taken from the safe. Between that and my pistol, I felt somewhat well-armed. Besides, I knew Frankie had an arsenal inside the walls of her safe houses, should I want to upgrade to something capable of taking out an entire platoon.

"Reconsider. After the week we've had, you're the world's leading candidate for owning a shiny new AK. Or a rocket launcher."

"Perfect for a household with a kid running around," I said, staring out at a nighttime highway that seemed as cold and desolate as the surface of the moon. "Now tell me where the hell I'm going."

Frankie directed me to the nearest town, and from there to a bridge that spanned the Snake. We crossed into the darkness of Oregon, insects speckling our windshield in a gooey rain. After a few miles, Frankie ordered me to slow and turn left, onto a narrow dirt lane that wound its way through dense brush. Twice I had to slow so we could bump through dry creek-beds thick with rocks.

"It's ideal out here," Frankie said, sounding genuinely happy. "You better believe I have some kickass cameras on those hills to our left, watching this road."

"This the only way in or out?" I asked.

"There's a pathway out back of the house, but it's too narrow for a vehicle. This is the only real road, and believe me, we can make it a kill-box real fast."

"Perfect for a siege."

"That's why we're here and not at the other safe houses. This one's my castle."

Twenty minutes later, we reached Frankie's "castle." I expected a concrete bunker, maybe surrounded by a ten-foot wall and a minefield or two, but what came into view after the last hill was a modern two-story house, as if Frankie had paid a contractor to rip an average home out of a subdivision and plop it down in the middle of nowhere.

"I was expecting more," I told her as I parked my truck beside the Monkey Man's van, which was parked facing the road. No sign of the weirdo himself. Beyond the van sat a battered SUV, easily fifteen years old, that was surely one of Frankie's patented trick vehicles: hidden compartments for weapons and all kinds of special goods, and probably a tuned-up monster of an engine for quick getaways.

"Oh, don't you fret. I'll give you the tour."

The house smelled of incense and fried food. Every room looked like something out of a Swedish furniture catalog: blonde-wood chairs and tables, cute blue wallpaper, lamps of colored glass bent into funky shapes. We found Surfer Boy on the couch in the front living room, watching a Bruce Willis classic on his phone, a 12-gauge pump-action on the floor beside him. As we entered, he looked up, his eyes reddened from crying, and said: "Benedict?"

"Fine, last I checked." Frankie shrugged. "Well, as fine as you can be after getting shot. It's not fun. But he's a tough guy."

Surfer Boy nodded. "Good."

"Where's our gorilla friend?"

"On the roof. He took one of the sniper rifles up with him."

"Yeah, he likes to sleep up there with the damn thing. He take the one from the SUV?"

"No, the upstairs gun locker."

"Good, I might need one."

Meanwhile I drifted toward entranceway to the dining room, which had a table long enough to comfortably seat twelve. Another doorway to my left led to the kitchen, where a teakettle whistled a mournful tune. Janine appeared, a bright yellow mug in her hand, and smiled at me. "Hey."

"Hey yourself," I said, wrapping my arms around her, sinking my face into the side of her neck.

She leaned into me, her warmth familiar and comfortable. "How'd it go?"

I froze. How would she react if I told her that our house had been invaded by a few gunmen and a former federal prosecutor with a very bad offer?

Frankie saved me. "Fine," she said. "Some of Jake's old cop friends were lurking around, but they left."

"Cops?" Janine pushed away from me. "What did they…"

"They wanted to return my guns," I said. "They also said they were sorry for thinking I'd killed that girl."

"A cop actually apologized?"

"Not in so many words. But if they were still angry, they would've found an excuse to not return my gear," I said, heading for the fridge. The kitchen was narrow, barely wide enough for two people to pass one another, and outfitted with the latest in silvery appliances. It must have cost a fortune to ship all that stuff out into the wilderness. At the far end, a door with four deadbolts and a chain led to the backyard.

"We got some Bud," Frankie called from the living room, reading my mind.

"Excellent." I removed two beers from the humming fridge. Tucking one beneath my armpit, I backed toward the kitchen doorway, raising the other can as if I was a quarterback readying to pass. Frankie waved it off, though. Janine stood beside her, chewing a fingernail, and I wanted to tell her that it was okay, that I wasn't slipping back into my old ways when it came to alcohol. I only needed a quick hit of self-care.

"I brought you some books," I told my wife, who said nothing. Maybe she doubted my story about the cops. I was a good liar to everyone but her.

"Jake, come on, I'll give you the rest of the tour," Frankie said, leading me up the stairs to the second floor. One can went into my pocket, and I popped the tab on the second. The beer felt heavenly cool on my throat.

Upstairs featured three bedrooms, outfitted with queen-sized beds and large desks. More blue wallpaper, paired with thick white rugs and mirrors in golden frames. It wasn't Frankie's style at all, but maybe that was the point: other people were supposed to use this space, and not everyone loved my sister's all-black aesthetic.

"Really doesn't look like a fortress," I said.

"Got guns in the walls, plus some cash. The front and back doors are lined with steel, the glass in the windows is bullet-resistant, and we have sensors all over the place. Trust me, we're good here, you worrywart."

We passed a bathroom with a deep and inviting tub. Despite my liberal application of deodorant at the hotel, I could still smell my funk, which meant it was ten times worse to everyone around me. I needed a long soak before crawling into bed with Janine for a day or two of beautiful, restorative sleep...

"Laptop's downstairs," Frankie said. "We should look up Karen's target."

I groaned.

"Don't give me that shit. Duty calls." She led me downstairs to the dining room, retrieving a slim laptop from a shelf on the way. Janine was no longer in the kitchen, but I wasn't worried. She often liked to sip her tea or wine in the open air, underneath the stars.

Once we sat down, Frankie opened the computer and typed a few commands, then hissed through her teeth. I moved so I could see the screen over her shoulder. Her open browser window framed a black kid, no more than twelve years old, offering a gap-toothed grin for the camera. He could have been one of my daughter's classmates. "Is that him?" I asked.

Frankie clicked, and the kid's image disappeared, replaced by an official-looking form. No doubt one of the government databases she could access, thanks to the bribes she seeded to various gray bureaucrats. "That's him," she sighed.

I almost dropped my beer. "That bitch wants us to kill a kid?"

14

"Sure seems like it." Frankie kept clicking through her browser's tabs, revealing pages from social networks, government databases, newspaper stories. "And before you ask, yes, I'm a hundred percent sure it's the same person. There's only one person by that name in the entire state, and they're at the same address that Karen gave us."

"Who's Karen?" Janine asked behind me.

"Someone who's not a problem yet," Frankie said, "although they could be."

"Who is she?" Janine said, louder, pushing past me into the dining room.

"She was with the cops at the house," I said, mangling the narrative a bit. "She's Ted Baker's sister. She was also a prosecutor at one point."

"The fuck was she doing with the cops?" Janine perched on Frankie's shoulder, reading the form on the screen. "Who's this...Anthony McKee?"

Frankie side-eyed a message to me: *come clean?*

I shrugged. Sooner or later, Janine would probably find out anyway.

"She showed up separately from the cops," Frankie said, which technically wasn't a lie. "She hated her brother, and she's willing to make sure that nothing about us or his sick little game ever gets out, but in exchange she wants us to do something horrible."

Janine crossed her arms over her chest. "How'd she find out about that stupid game?"

"Ted had some files about us that automatically uploaded to some kind of cloud server, which she has the password for," Frankie said. "At least, that's the bullshit she tried selling us. But the fact that she showed up at your house means she knows too much, in any case."

"And what's this Anthony have to do with it?"

"She wants us to kill him," I said.

Janine bent slightly to read the screen. "Says here Anthony is...twelve."

"Don't worry, we're not going to hurt him," Frankie said. "And granted, I've only been on the case for a grand total of twenty minutes, but nothing I've drawn up so far shows why an ex-prosecutor would want a boy killed."

"That's horrible," Janine said. "On that form, that box under relatives, it says he had a brother who died?"

"Right." Frankie copied the brother's name, Ewan McKee, and pasted it into the search bar in a new browser tab. She hit enter, and a slew of links popped into view:

BOISE YOUTH SHOT AND KILLED
POLICE DEPARTMENT CLAIMS JUSTIFIED SHOOTING

The top link was an article in the *Idaho Statesman*, dated six months previous. Eighteen-year-old boy shot in his car while driving home. A nice boy who played for his school's football team and never had an unkind word for anyone, according to the friends and neighbors quoted in the piece. I racked my brain, trying to remember if I'd heard of this case—police shootings are rare in Boise, which is generally considered a safe city—but nothing came to mind. I tended to only focus on crimes when I had to chase down the scumbags who'd committed them.

"Click on a bunch," I told her.

Wikipedia and a few old news links revived the facts buried in my memory: Ewan had been driving down 9th Street in downtown Boise on a hot July night when an officer named Bruce Melinek pulled him over for reasons that seemed unclear. In the back seat of Ewan's vehicle sat Anthony. The officer told the investigators that he was approaching the driver's side window when he saw Ewan make an "aggressive maneuver" that "put him in fear of his life." Drawing his service pistol, he fired ten shots, two of which struck Ewan in the neck and chest.

One of those bullets snapped right over Anthony's head. If the kid had been three inches taller, he would have been killed or maimed.

The officer was put on administrative leave, pending an investigation, but was eventually cleared of charges. The review board concluded that he had legitimately feared for his life, despite the lack of a weapon in Ewan's vehicle. None of the articles mentioned the name of Bruce Melinek's partner in the patrol vehicle that night, nor did Karen pop up. Ewan's adopted parents spent the next two years threatening a lawsuit, but nothing came of it.

"So Anthony's brother was shot," Frankie said. "Could mean something. Could mean nothing, except that ol' Bruce was a scared little bitch."

"When did Karen stop being a prosecutor?" Janine asked.

"Way before this." Frankie returned to the search screen and typed in Karen's full name, then clicked on the first result: a short Wikipedia page, all of its details obviously cut-and-pasted from some kind of official bio. It told us that Karen had retired as a prosecutor five years ago.

"So it's not a case she would have dealt with," I said.

"Even if she was still on the government teat, she might not have touched it at all," Frankie said. "Her interest was in big cases. Guns, wholesale drug shipments, stuff you use to make a name for yourself."

"So maybe the dead brother isn't a factor," I said.

"I presume Karen didn't tell you why she wants the kid

dead," Janine said.

Frankie shook her head.

"I'm obviously more in the dark than you are about this," Janine continued, "but here's the question in my mind: if she expected you to kill this poor kid, wouldn't she also expect you to do some research beforehand? Maybe ask the kid why a big politician wants him shot?"

"She thinks we're stupid," I offered.

"Nope." Frankie closed her eyes and squeezed the bridge of her nose. "Janine's right. There's something weird going on here. I mean, something weirder than all the other weird stuff."

"I'm still not sure about that," I said. "Look, Karen's rich. She's also in law enforcement. I'm not saying she's dumb, but I'm saying people like that tend to look at a lot of people like animals. Maybe she thinks we'll walk up and shoot the kid and not ask questions because we just want this over with. She's arrogant, not weird or plotting anything else. That's what I think, at least."

"Well, there's only one way to find out," Frankie said, slapping the laptop closed. "We got to ask the kid."

15

It was a bad night. As much as my body needed rest, every time I slipped toward sleep, my traitorous brain sprinted into the basement of my subconscious and hit play on the messiest, bloodiest movies it could find. It was like when I first returned from Iraq, and my dreams for a year afterward were filled with bloody limbs tossed onto blackened sand, children without heads and women screaming. Now, when my eyes closed, it was the same bloody chaos—only it was the streets of Boise, my friends and neighbors wailing in pain as their shattered bodies leaked red onto the pavement.

I resisted tossing and turning, knowing it wouldn't help. Beside me, Janine slept peacefully, for which I was thankful. At least she was getting some rest.

I drifted off. When I awoke again, I noticed how my fingers stuck to the sheets. In the gray light of dawn, I saw the white cotton around my waist stained with bits of red.

I touched one of the red spots. It was blood, nearly dried.

Oh crap, not again.

In Iraq, I took some shrapnel to the legs and arms and neck. After pulling out the bigger pieces, the surgeons decided some of the smaller slivers weren't worth the digging. Every six months or so, my body ejected some metal bits on its own.

I felt the sheets until my thumb snagged on a tiny sharpness that felt like a pencil tip. Then I ran my hands over my body until I touched what felt like a sore on my hip. Now I knew why that spot had itched for weeks. What I had assumed was an annoying bug bite was actually my muscles deciding enough was enough with this artifact from my past.

I dropped the shrapnel into my empty water glass on the nightstand and headed to the bathroom to shower and bandage myself up. The scalding-hot water felt good on the muscles of my back and legs, which threatened to stiffen up after all the running and gunning. The penalty for getting old, I guess. After patching the hole in my hip, I raided Frankie's medicine cabinet for a pain pill.

Wearing only my jeans, I headed downstairs. Through the kitchen windows, I spied Frankie standing on the back lawn, sipping a giant mug of coffee. Pouring myself a cup of high-octane caffeine from the burbling pot on the counter, I headed outside to join her.

"Hey," she said, glancing in my direction as the door slammed behind me. Based on the dark circles around her eyes, she hadn't slept at all. Then again, she almost always looked like she had been awake for the past three days.

"We okay?" I asked.

"Yeah, I'm admiring the beauty of Oregon," she said, jabbing her mug at the stark landscape behind the house, where the rolling lawn gave way to fields of yellow grass. Despite the early hour, the heat prickled my skin, drawing sweat from my neck. Maybe two hundred yards away, a crooked barbed-wire fence wound its way along what looked like a cliff or hillside, given how the land fell away beyond.

"What's back there?" I asked.

"There's a valley," she said, waving her mug in either direction. "A good moat. It's narrow but deep. River at the bottom. It extends probably five miles east and west."

"Could someone cross it?"

"Sure, but we'd see them coming. I have cameras back there, too. Plus, it's overgrown and filled with snakes. It'd take you forever."

"And what's beyond that?" I said, pointing into the shimmering distance, where dry hills seemed to hump into infinity.

"Nearest town's fifteen miles away. There's a dirt road, marked private, that loops around to the main road. A hot spring that's not on any websites, thankfully, or I'd be shooting stray teens like deer every other week." She smirked.

"Janine likes hot springs."

"But she hates rattlers. Trust me, it's hard bushwhacking to get there. Like I said last night, this is a real fortress, bro. You hungry?"

"Yeah."

"Good. I sent Surfer Boy and the Monkey Man drove to the market for some breakfast stuff. I told them I could protect your sleeping asses until you got back. Let's head inside, because I need more coffee."

"You talk to your guys up north?"

"Yeah, right before you came down. Keith's babbling about weed and space aliens. Don't ask me how he's still high after this long. Maybe he's sober, and his brain's a broken toy. I told them to waterboard him if he got too annoying."

As we took seats in the dining room, our mugs refilled, she said: "Have I told you this morning that you look like shit?"

"I don't think so."

"Because you look like shit."

"That makes two of us."

"Yeah, but I make looking like shit look good. Besides, I've been thinking about our situation."

I took a sip of coffee. My second cup tasted as much like boiled ink as the first, but the caffeine hit my veins like an express train, and for that I was thankful. "Did you come to any amazing conclusions?"

"We're screwed." She chuckled. "What else is new."

"Seriously."

"Seriously, we're not going to corner a kid and start interrogating him. If we tried swearing him to silence, he'd still tell someone, then we'd have the cops all over us. And given Karen's connections to every pig in the state—"

"Hey now."

"What?"

"You know I don't like it when you say 'pig.'"

"Yeah? Why's that? Because law enforcement has always treated you so nicely?"

"I was almost an MP."

"Sure, but that's the military. I got nothing but respect for soldiers. Some of my best guys are ex-Army."

"Anyway." I slammed my mug onto the table a little too heavily. "Okay, if we don't talk to the kid, what do we do?"

Frankie rolled her eyes. "Bro, don't you get it? We don't bother with the kid. Talk to the parents. They'll know more anyway."

"And you don't think they'll go right to the cops?"

"Are you kidding? The cops shot their other kid."

"Then what's our play?"

"We fake like we're reporters. Follow-up for an old article. Probe for some kind of Karen connection."

"You think they'll buy it?"

She saluted me with her coffee cup. "Well, I don't know if your redneck ass could pass for a journalist, but let me assure you, it's a ruse I've used before. I have a couple of business cards that say 'reporter.'"

"What if they search for your byline online? See you haven't written anything?"

"Don't make me throw this coffee at you. It'll burn."

"What?"

"They're real business cards, dumbass. Belong to a freelance journalist who quit the game maybe two, three years back. She moved to Seattle, works in a coffee shop. I guess that pays better. Anyway, there aren't many photos of her online, and she kind of looked like me, anyway."

She tried to keep her face impassive, hoping I would forget, but I winked and said: "Oh, that's right, that was your ex."

"Don't."

"Don't what?"

"Don't bring it up. Please." She raised her mug to her lips, blocking part of her face, but not quickly enough to hide the flicker of pain. My stomach dropped with shame. Frankie hooked up frequently with men and women, tossing them aside once she was done, never to be mentioned again. I had no idea that one had left a scar.

"Sorry," I said, and meant it.

"You better be." She grimaced. "I'm not a total psychopath, remember?"

"Just a partial one?"

"Oh, you're so hilarious."

"I really am sorry."

"I'll accept your apology if you take me to Fanci Freez after we interview these parents."

"And when are we doing that?"

"Soon as the cavalry gets back with breakfast."

As if on cue, the faint rumble of a car rolling up the gravel driveway. I stood, intending to intercept Benedict at the door—if he was carrying anything delicious in his bag from the store, I wanted first dibs before Frankie and her all-consuming black hole of a stomach. I was facing away from the windows as I rose, but the expression on Frankie's face said something was very wrong, even before she shoved her chair back and stood.

I crouched on instinct, spinning on my back foot. Through the window's slats and dusty screen, I saw a green SUV bouncing its way toward the house, its heavy wheels churning up dust. I didn't recognize the vehicle.

Gripping her chair by the back, Frankie slammed it into the wall, grunting as she did so. The chair's heavy wooden legs punched through the wallpaper and cheap drywall in two places. Tossing the chair aside, she tore a larger hole with her hands, revealing three UMPs dangling on pegs in the gaps between the studs. Her face and forearms dusted white, she pulled out one of the weapons and tossed it to me, then retrieved another.

"Jake?" Janine called from upstairs. "What's going on?"

"Get in the tub," I called back. "Get low."

"Oh shit, not again." Janine's footsteps loud in the hallway as she headed for the bathroom.

Reaching into the hole, Frankie tossed four extended magazines onto the table. I snatched one up and slotted it into my submachine gun, chambered a round, and clicked off the safety. "Friends of yours?" I asked.

"No idea," she said, loading her own weapon. "Head out the back."

"Shouldn't we lock down in here? Steel doors and bulletproof glass?"

"Won't help us if they set the place on fire."

"Might be a Jehovah's Witness."

"Oh, then we'll definitely make sure they don't come back." Tucked down, Frankie sprinted for the front door. I took a left through the kitchen and out the back door, moving as low and fast as I could, my world tight over my barrel. Unless you counted the rabbit bounding its way toward the sagging fence that marked the property line, the yard was empty of threats. Without pausing I pivoted right, keeping the side of the house at arm's length as I moved toward the front. Sometimes a round will skip along a wall, so you want to leave a gap rather than press yourself against it.

The SUV's engine cut out. Frankie shouted: "What the hell?"

I took a knee as I reached the corner. From this angle I had a clear view of the driveway. The SUV had parked broadside, blocking Frankie's car and my truck. Two men stood in front of it, looking relaxed despite Frankie presumably pointing a weapon at them, but I couldn't see her.

I darted my head around the corner. No sign of Frankie. I assumed she had taken a position inside the front doorway, using the jamb for partial cover as she aimed through the screen door. There were no lights in the front hallway, and strong sun beating down on the two men would make it hard to see inside the house.

I recognized one of the men: my old friend Jim, last seen freaking out in my kitchen when he thought my sister shot one of his men. He was dressed for success in a pair of faded jeans and a green polo shirt with a slightly frayed collar. The shirt was a little small and his hairy gut seeped below the hem, spilling over his belt buckle. He had no weapons visible, but that didn't mean anything. The jeans were loose enough to hide a backup pistol on his calf.

The man next to him, on the other hand, was a real peacock: hair as black and shiny as a helmet, swept tight against a narrow skull. He wore a snakeskin jacket over a button-down black shirt, paired with black trousers. Large sunglasses with pinkish frames hid his eyes, and an unfiltered, unlit cigarette jittered in the corner of his mouth. I didn't recognize him, but when you thought about it, I had only dragged a small portion of the Treasure Valley's criminals back to jail at one point or another.

Frankie must have recognized him, though, because she snarled: "Boz, you shit."

Boz grinned, his cigarette tipping upwards at a jaunty angle that reminded me of photographs of Franklin D. Roosevelt with his cigarette holder. "Hey, baby," he called out. "It's been a long time. Don't shoot me, okay?"

Boz. The name was vaguely familiar, and it took me a moment to remember long-ago Frankie breathing the name like a curse as she snapped a half-finished cigarette out an open car window, into the night, as we roared out of Boise and into the hills. Yes: Boz was another ex, one I hadn't met, another gunrunner or criminal of some sort, but one who kept a low profile despite dressing like a Vegas pimp.

"Bro?" Frankie called.

"Here," I called back, making sure that I had my gunsights slotted between Jim's eyes. Aim small, miss small. I worried that

94

these guys had arrived with backup of some kind, one or two guys circling behind the house right now. Why else would Boz seem relaxed as he tilted in my direction, raising a hand in a loose salute?

"Seriously, we're just here to talk," Boz said. "We're all playing on Karen's team, okay?"

"Bro," Frankie said. "Moving."

"Move," I called back.

The screen door slammed open, and Frankie darted through low, UMP aimed at Boz. Fast down the porch steps, then a wide swing to the right, staying clear of my line of fire, before she angled toward the pair. "I want to see some hands," she told them.

They raised their hands, Jim's cheeks reddening, Boz smirking. Lowering her weapon against her hip, Frankie patted down Jim's armpits, back, crotch, and ankles before shoving him forward, away from the SUV. As he stumbled across the lawn, she moved to Boz, her hand darting inside his jacket, along his waistline, down his arms and legs. "Oh, yeah, baby," Boz said, nodding enthusiastically. "You know what I like."

"Cut it." Frankie tapped the UMP's barrel against his chin. "I will feed the grass with your brains."

"I don't get why you're so irate," Boz said. "I mean, don't you still have my espresso machine?"

"Remember, I know which knee is your bad one." Did a smile flicker in the corner of her lips? It was hard to tell at this distance. I stood, making sure that Jim stayed locked on me as I walked toward him, never lowering my weapon. Maybe they did want to talk, but my paranoia had kept me alive this long, and it was telling me that something very bad was happening here.

"Jim," I said. "I want you to get down on the ground, inter-lace your hands behind your head, okay?" I didn't have handcuffs or any rope to tie him up with. I thought about yelling into the house for Janine, asking her to bring out whatever she could find, but she was safer in the tub.

Jim followed orders, his knees popping as he did so. "Guess we're making a habit of this," I said.

"You had to rub it in," Boz said behind me. "You might regret that later."

Jim cursed into the grass.

"You wanted to talk," Frankie said, stepping away from Boz. "So talk. And make it quick, it's way too early in the morning for this crap."

"You always were a night person." Boz began to lower his hands. "Can I get my lighter?"

"Is that same one you used to have, the gold one with the naked lady?"

"You made me toss that one, remember? New one's a silver Zippo."

"Sure, yeah."

Boz drew that Zippo from his pocket and torched the tip of his cigarette. Blasting smoke from his nostrils, he said: "Karen told us she gave you an assignment, right? She didn't tell us what it was, but she said it was important—"

"Wait, rewind. How are you involved with Karen?"

"That's way too long a story for right now." Boz glanced behind him, down the driveway. Was he worried about Frankie's people showing up? Or was he looking for his own backup?

"How many others?" I asked Jim.

Jim tilted his head toward me. "What?"

"Don't tell me it's only you two."

"Hey, war hero, we wanted to talk, nothing more." Boz hissed smoke. "We could have come in shooting. Or burned the house down before you realized what was up. But we didn't, and we didn't harm your guys back at the store, just put a screwdriver in their tire when they were inside."

"This thing with Karen," Frankie said, her eyes flicking at me for a microsecond. "We're doing it tonight. Show up here at nine, if you want to come along. That's why you're here, right?

You're going to make sure we do our jobs?"

"Something like that."

"How did you find us, anyway?"

"We came up here once, remember?"

"No. I thought I bought it after we broke up."

"Nah, it was before. It still smelled like fresh paint." Boz pointed at the front of the house. "I remember asking why you didn't want to paint it black, and you said that you were trying to be a little girly."

"Don't make me hit you." Wonder of wonders, Frankie blushed slightly.

Boz winked at me. "I know all those deep, dark secrets."

"Karen's thing," Frankie said, anxious to change the subject. "I'm warning you now, it's going to be unpleasant."

"More unpleasant than Montana?"

"Don't joke." Frankie walked backward, her UMP barrel lowered.

"I guess you can get up," I told Jim, who promptly squirmed to a crouch, wincing in that way of older men with aching joints. I still didn't feel sorry for him, especially since he offered me a look of pure death as he finally made it to his feet.

"See you then," Frankie said. Did I detect a certain wistfulness in her voice? Maybe Boz did, too, because he removed his sunglasses, revealing dark eyes that looked like holes punched through his skull.

"What?" he said. "You're not going to invite us in for breakfast? Your famous burnt eggs? C'mon, nightingale, I thought we had something real."

Frankie pulled the trigger. The gunshot echoed off the hills, paired with the passenger window of Boz's SUV shattering. Boz flinched, his cigarette tumbling to the dirt. Still in a crouch, Jim squealed in fear.

"Oops," Frankie said. "Did I do that?"

16

"Nightingale?" I said. "Really?"

"Don't you dare." For the past fifteen minutes, once Boz and Jim fled and we returned to the house, Frankie had refused to look in my direction. Now we sat at the dining room table. Based on how she kept her eyes fixed on the wood, the patterns in the oak must have been absolutely fascinating.

"Or what?" I smiled. "You'll kill me?"

"Nah, I'll shoot you in the calf. Hurts like a bitch, and you never walk right again."

The living room windows framed Frankie's men as they made a big show of walking back and forth on the lawn, pistols jammed in their belts, properly humiliated by their failure to protect her. Janine, still irate after taking cover in the bathroom, was upstairs reading a book. For the moment, it was just us siblings on the first floor.

Neither of us liked having these heart-to-heart discussions. We came from a family where a refusal to show emotion was considered high virtue. Janine had pried my heart open a bit over the years, but Frankie had nobody to squeeze the emotions from her.

"It's okay to be vulnerable, you know," I said, cringing at how awkward the words sounded. "If you can't be vulnerable with me, who else is there?"

"Spare me the Oprah crap. It's not that. You know I talk about my relationships with you." She raised her head. Much to my surprise, her eyes were wide, soft. "Boz, he was…different."

"I could see that. Nobody would walk outside dressed like that unless they had an enormous pair of balls."

"No, as in…" She sighed. "It could have been something."

"But you never told me about him."

"Yeah, because it could have been something. I wanted to be sure before I introduced him around, you know? This was also when you were still in Iraq."

"What happened?"

Frankie swallowed. "He wanted kids. I didn't."

"Oh."

"It wasn't a bad breakup. There wasn't any screaming or yelling. We just…drifted."

My heart broke for her, but we also had a situation on our hands. Leaning forward, I asked: "Who is he? I mean, what does he do?"

"He used to deal guns. That's how we met. Different territories, or I'd probably have killed him before I tried talking to him. He ran rifles between Oregon and California, mostly to the gangs down in Oakland."

"Then he did something else?"

"Yeah, it was getting too heavy for him, even when we were together. A bad night in Oakland, he lost a bunch of people. I have no idea what he did next, though, because we broke up. Obviously, he got jammed up with Karen."

"Do you think he still has feelings for you?"

She bared her teeth at me. "Gee, I didn't quite get around to asking him, what with everyone pointing guns at each other and all."

"It's an important question. Whatever you feel for him, we might have to kill him before this is over."

"You think I don't know that?" She had resumed staring at the table. "Man, this is totally screwed up. I told him that I didn't want to bring a baby into this world, into this life we have, and you know what he said? He said we'd find a way, that things could be different."

"You didn't believe him?"

"No, I did. I have money. I'm smart. We could have quit and gone legit, somehow. I just...I didn't want to quit the life. It's what I know, and I'm good at it. I felt like a kid would drag me down somehow."

"And now?"

She ran her nails along the wood. "I don't know. I have too many mouths to feed, too much going on. Maybe if I unwound everything, I could quit. I'll have to do it at some point, before my body gives out."

I reached over and wrapped two of my fingers around her thumb. She closed my fingers in her hand and squeezed. "Whatever you decide, I'm here," I said.

"It's not like you have a choice." Pulling away, she checked her watch. "First I'm going to call as many of my guys as possible to come lock this place down. Then we're going to go ask that kid's parents why the state's most powerful lady wants him dead."

17

A decade ago, the drive to downtown Boise was a quick one. During rush hour, you might hit some traffic along I-84—especially if a fender bender closed down a lane or three—but otherwise you could almost always keep your odometer pegged at seventy or eighty until you hit the off-ramp (if you drove like me, that is).

But over the past few years, as more folks moved into the Treasure Valley, the traffic into Boise grew more clogged. This morning was no exception. We sat in a bumper-to-bumper snarl, the phone clipped to the dashboard of Frankie's SUV telling us that our destination was still eight miles away—and it would take us more than an hour to reach it, if all the cars around us kept hitching along at a geezer's pace. I knew that, as soon as we started moving at a reasonable speed again, our projected time of arrival would drop to a few minutes. Nonetheless, Frankie had begun to glance at the phone as if it was her worst enemy, and I feared her rage would build to the point where she threw the damn thing out the window.

We have some serious anger-management issues in our family, to put it mildly.

"A while back," I said, hoping to distract her, "I was talking to this dude who moved here from California. He said that he sold his house in San Francisco for a couple of million, decided to buy a place over in Warm Springs Mesa. He told me that, as he was moving, he was fantasizing about never having to deal with a California traffic jam ever again."

"Was this your neighbor? The guy we killed?"

One of our neighbors, Rob, was a rich guy from California who was good friends with Ted Baker. I hadn't thought about him much since Frankie shot him in the head, but I realized now that his death was a huge problem. If the cops figured out who he was—difficult, since Frankie had set Rob's body on fire—they would focus on me.

"No," I said, "although that's a problem we might have to deal with at some point."

"This other California guy, he was sorely disappointed at Idaho's traffic, I take it?"

"Yeah. He gets here, he finds himself sitting in the exact crap he was trying to escape from."

"I heard it's like that all over the West. Denver, Salt Lake, here. All these fucking California folks trying to escape, they're bringing all their problems to us."

"Not sure there's anything we can do about it."

"Move out further. All those crackpots up north, with their compounds? Most of the time, I think they're insane, although they're good customers. But when I'm sitting in this shit," she pounded the steering wheel, "I start to think maybe they have a point. Screw civilization."

"That's pretty stark."

"Nah, I'm serious. What's civilization ever got us? Traffic jams, nukes, assholes on the internet."

"But also potato chips, whiskey, video games, and good books."

"Potato chips?"

"What?"

"You're considering that the peak of civilization? Snack food?"

"No. I mean, if I had to rank them, I'd definitely put whiskey first. Followed by books."

She grinned. "Well, that's a little more civilized."

"Before there was civilization, everyone was also dead by

thirty, remember. You'd probably have given birth ten times by the time you were twenty, if you lived."

I was edging to a dangerous line there, bringing up babies, even hypothetical cave-babies. But Frankie seemed into it, if only because it distracted her from the unmoving traffic. "Hey, ten kids, that's the beginnings of a nice little army. I could have conquered the ancient world in no time."

"Should have known you'd think like that."

"If I'd conquered the ancient world, I could have fixed a lot of things early. Trust me, there'd be no such thing as a traffic jam today. Not sure *how* the ancient version of me would accomplish that, but we'd get it done."

The phone beeped, and the onscreen map flickered, recalibrating. The traffic was loosening about a quarter of a mile ahead, the cars around us inching forward. Frankie adjusted her grip on the wheel, leaning back in her seat. "After everything that's happened this week, I'm also not big on humanity in general."

"I've never been big on it. Side effect of the whole bounty hunting thing. But what those assholes tried to do to us, it's not normal."

"No, it is. I hate to say it, but it is." She eased on the gas, bumping us forward ten feet before traffic froze again. "Maybe not the game itself—dragging people into the woods to hunt them is pretty weird—but the cruelty underneath it, that's human beings in a nutshell."

"Well." As much as I wanted to disagree with her, I'd seen too much misery and cruelty to do so. I remembered bursts of white phosphorus drifting from the night sky over Fallujah, smoky tentacles of death that burned everything beneath, and shuddered. This car suddenly seemed too cold, too small, too loaded with gasoline that would char us to black husks like the Iraqis I would find after a bombardment, and I recognized the panic attack coming on and I knew how to stop it, lean forward and breathe deep and tell myself that everything was okay, but everything wasn't okay, we were—

"Bro?" Frankie's warm hand on my shoulder as I leaned forward.

"I am okay," I said through clenched teeth. "I am frosty."

"No, you're not." Her hand drifted to my chin, gently forcing my head up. "Look at me."

I did, trying to fix her with my hardest possible stare. As much as I loved my sister, I knew she hated weakness in all forms. And despite all that we'd gone through together, I feared she would somehow think less of me if she saw me like this.

"I have no idea what you've gone through," she said. "And I'll never comprehend it, not really. But you're never alone, okay? You will always have me, and I don't care about anything else."

I swallowed hard, my heart pounding loud in my ears. "Okay."

"Don't 'okay' me. Repeat: 'My sister is always there for me.'"

"My sister is always there for me."

"Good." Leaning forward, she kissed my cheek. "Use that as your mantra."

This was my second panic attack in three days. Not good, but maybe not the worst considering what I had endured. Under normal circumstances, I faced race and reliable triggers: fireworks (the Fourth of July was always hell), the smell of burning gasoline, and the sound of jackhammers would all put me in a state of intense alert, heart slamming against my ribs, every nerve wired for combat. News stories about struggling veterans always made me cry uncontrollably. These rapid panic attacks were new territory, though, and I hoped they would disappear after life returned to its old rhythms.

If we survived, of course.

Behind us, a car honked, the driver leaning on the horn. The truck front of us had moved up another twenty feet, and a car to our left was trying to edge its way into our lane. Frankie growled low in her throat and smacked the glove compartment open, revealing a large black .45 automatic.

"What are you doing?" I asked.

"Car behind us," Frankie said, glancing into the rearview mirror, "and that jerk trying to come on the left here? Both have California plates."

"I meant with the gun."

Frankie zipped down her window and dangled her arm out, pistol in her hand. The honking behind us stopped. The car to our left jerked hard into its own lane, the driver's mouth wide with panic. "Exercising my open-carry rights," Frankie said, locking eyes with the driver. "Expressing my undying love of the Second Amendment."

"Um, okay." Idaho might have loved the Second Amendment as much as Frankie, but in my experience, even the biggest gun lovers had a tendency to panic when you started waving a firearm around. "What if they call the cops? Or pull their own gun?"

Returning the pistol to the glove compartment, Frankie rolled her window up. "Because we're taking side streets. I'm through with this highway shit."

After tooting her horn twice, she angled into the lane to our right, where two cars did their best to create a gap for us to pass through, onto the shoulder. Once there, Frankie stomped on the gas, rocketing us toward the exit in the distance. I tried to look calm while clutching my seatbelt.

"Relax," she said. "There are no cops around."

"I don't want you to get a ticket."

The exit was blessedly close. I knew it led onto the surface streets behind a shopping complex (featuring that holy trinity of American commerce: Walmart, Lowe's, and a movie theater), and from there we could take Overland Road into Boise proper. Frankie would spend some time cruising down random streets, until she was sure nobody was following us, but this was still faster than the highway.

"If we did get pulled over," Frankie said, as we hit the ramp at high speed, "I wouldn't worry so much about a traffic ticket. I'd be way more concerned about the cop glimpsing all the weaponry in the back."

I twisted in my seat for a better look at our cargo bay, almost yelling: "What did you bring?"

18

Frankie's SUV had a hidden compartment beneath the floor in the back. It was deep and wide enough for a UMP, a pump-action 12-gauge shotgun, and a McMillan TAC-338, a sniper rifle with enough stopping power to kill effectively at a thousand meters.

"Did you know," Frankie said, pointing to the boxes of ammunition lined up beside the weapons, "that the TAC is responsible for three of the top five sniper kills? Some dude used one to kill an ISIS fighter at three thousand feet or whatever. Crazy."

"Why in the everloving fuck are you driving around with that?" I had fired the TAC-338 a few times in Iraq. It had a lot of kick. The box magazines held five .338 rounds, but if you were good at marksmanship, you only needed one.

"Client wanted one for hunting. I asked him why, and he said it's the gun that Bradley Cooper used in *American Sniper*. I was like, dude, that's a dumbass reason, you got to respect hardware like this."

"Then what happened?"

"Then I didn't sell it to him. Told him it was too much gun." Closing the compartment, she returned the carpet to its previous position, then placed the first aid kit and a cheap windbreaker on top.

We had parked on West State Street, in front of a small white house with blue trim and a wide porch. The rest of the block was surrendering, house by house, to the overwhelming power of money. I remembered that the far corner had once featured a gas station, now replaced by a construction site surrounded by bright orange mesh and a wall of cheap plywood. On that wall, the developers had posted an architectural drawing of a three-story condo, all smooth concrete and glass.

"California," I told Frankie, who laughed.

Frankie led the way up the walk to the small house. We were nearly to the porch when the front door opened and a wizened old man with a thin, wrinkled neck walked into the sunlight. "We don't want no cops around," he informed us in a gravelly voice.

"Excuse me?" Frankie asked.

"No cops," the man said. "We talked to you people enough."

Frankie and I were dressed in jeans and plain T-shirts, no holsters, no badges or lanyards. Nothing about us screamed "police" except maybe our sunglasses. "We're not cops," Frankie said.

"Or private detectives. Some of those folks been around, too." The man's cheeks reddened, and he spoke louder, his hand slapping the air for emphasis.

"We're none of the above," Frankie said. "We just want to talk about Karen."

The man's brows furrowed. "Who?"

I said: "Karen Baker, the former prosecutor, you know her?" If the kid lived here, as Frankie assumed, then this man must have been his grandfather. And the old man talked about cops as if they swung by the house on a regular basis.

"Karen..." The man took a step backward, toward his door. "Who are you people?"

"It's about your grandson," I said. "We think Karen has some kind of interest in him."

"I got no grandson," the man said. "I got a son, still, but he's got no grandkids. Too young."

Squinting at the man, I realized he was at least three decades younger than I'd thought at first. Despite the gray in his hair, his face was relatively wrinkle-free, and his eyes were clear. His shoulders were stooped, but his spine was straight. I had seen this sort of thing many times: people aged by grief or trauma into shadows of their former selves.

I got a son, still.

I felt the edges of what was happening here. It wasn't fully clear yet, but I had the sense to clasp my hands over my stomach, like someone waiting at the edge of a burial plot. "Sorry for your loss," I said.

"That's all right." The man's face softened. "Why you think I got a grandson?"

"My mistake," I said. "But we want to talk to you about Karen. She's maybe key to what we're working on. My name is Jake, by the way. This is," I struggled for the name of Frankie's ex. "Regina."

"We're freelance journalists," Frankie said, and drew one of her ex's cards from her pocket. "Doing a follow-up feature."

"Feature?"

"It's about police shootings in Idaho, and Karen's possible involvement in how those cases ended up." A car honked a few blocks away, making me realize how exposed we were, standing on the sidewalk like this. "Can we come in? We don't want to take up too much of your time."

The door behind the man creaked open, and a woman stepped out. Whatever trauma had hit their family, it had impacted her far less than her husband, I thought. Her hair was dark and dry, flowing over her shoulders, and she moved with the easy grace of a former dancer.

As she stepped onto the porch, though, I had a better look at her eyes. Whatever had made her husband into an old man had also cored out her soul. She looked like civilians who had suffered through two weeks of heavy artillery fire in the desert: total shell shock.

She had a pistol in her hand, a small revolver that looked ill-maintained. She said to her husband: "Who are these people?"

"Journalists. Doing a story," he replied, never looking at her. The woman snorted. "We don't want to talk."

"Look," Frankie glanced around, evidently feeling as exposed as I was. "We don't want to take up much of your time here. But we've come across several references to Karen Baker, a federal prosecutor, and we wanted to know if she was a factor in your son's death. We want to help."

The woman said: "Factor?"

I sighed. "She might have tried to cover it up somehow. What happened."

To my amazement, the woman started laughing, deep and rich, rocking back on her heels as she did so. At least her pistol barrel kept pointed at the ground, or I would have been worried. Her husband—that's what I assumed he was—bowed his head, a hand covering his eyes.

After a few moments, her laughter dried up. Taking an enormous breath, she said: "Well, that's irony for you. No way I let you in the house, but come on around to the back, through that side gate. No harm in sharing what we know."

The husband sighed and waved for us to follow him around the side of the house, where a waist-high chain-link gate blocked access to an overgrown backyard. I tensed as we approached, ready for the sound of barking. As a bounty hunter, it was good policy for me to assume that every house had a dog or two. But no furry protectors greeted us.

Frankie was nervous, and with good reason. Staying on the street made us nervous because of potential witnesses; a random backyard, private and out of sight, was a good place for an ambush. As we followed the husband through the gate, Frankie tapped my elbow with hers. When I looked around, she tugged at the left leg of her jeans, pulling up the cuff enough to reveal the bottom edge of her ankle holster.

I winced. A backup gun wasn't much, but it was something, at least.

The wife, having come through the house, met us in the back

with a six-pack of soda, which she dumped on the glass table set in the middle of the grass. She sat down, drawing her revolver from her waistband as she did so, placing it on the table within easy reach. Her husband took the seat beside her, while we dropped into the two seats on the table's far side.

I scanned the yard. At one point, the couple had managed a bountiful garden against the rear fence, at least three rows of tomatoes and squash and peppers. Now the plants had over-grown their boundaries, forming a tangle of branches and vines and misshapen fruits. The fence itself was falling in, the wood warped by too many hot summers and brutal winters.

"My name's Jill, by the way," the wife said, pulling a soda free and yanking the tab. With a nod to her husband: "And that's Ricky. And you are?"

"I'm Jake," I said, extending my hand for a shake. "And that's Regina."

"You have some kind of identification? Showing you're journalists?"

Frankie slid Regina's card across the table. "Please feel free to Google my name. I have lots of bylines. I've been covering the crime beat off and on for years. Sometimes for the *States-man*, couple pieces in the *Weekly*."

"The *Weekly* is fake news," Ricky informed us. "Bunch of liberal trash."

"I like their music coverage," Jill said. "Your story's on police brutality? What's Karen's connection?"

"We're not totally sure." Frankie crossed her legs so the ankle with the backup pistol rested on her knee, within easy reach of her hand. "With your son's shooting, she may have pulled a string or two. Have you met her? Did you ever get the sense of any kind of interference?"

"Is he a journalist, too?" Jill pointed at me. "Does he have a card? Or bylines?"

"No, I'm the assistant, just getting into the profession," I said. "I'm watching how she does it, helping out, getting some tips."

"Anyway," Frankie said. "We had a meeting with a source within the Boise Police Department—you'll understand that I can't name him—and he mentioned your deceased son. Also Anthony."

A faint, metallic crinkle as Jill's fingers crunched the soda can. "Mentioned Ewan how?"

"That Karen had to clear things up," I said, uncomfortable with this chain of lies. Their son was in danger. Should we tell them to call the police? To flee? But that was the problem with Karen and her whole miserable family. She no doubt had influence with the police, and no place was safe from her reach.

Jill and Ricky glanced at each other. Ricky's throat worked for a long time before he said: "The officer who shot…"

"They dropped the charges against that officer, right? Bruce Melinek?" Frankie asked. She had taken out her phone, placed it on the table, and opened up an audio-recording app, just like a real reporter.

"They did." A single tear rolled down Jill's face, and she paused to wipe it away. "It was bullshit, let me tell you. The officer did everything wrong, and our little boy died as a result. Ewan was driving Anthony home from daycare and then…and then…"

Jill began to stand, seemed to think better of it, and crashed heavily into her chair again. Ricky reached out a hand to comfort her, but she slapped it away. The muscles in Ricky's face jumped as he tried to hold back his own sadness.

"I'm so sorry," I said. "I'm so, so sorry."

"Anthony," Ricky said, after he took a deep breath and held it for a second. "He was in the back seat of the car. Watched his brother die. He didn't talk for the longest time. Traumatized. We put him into therapy, which was so expensive, I had to get a second job to cover it…"

"Is he talking now?" Frankie asked.

Jill smiled. "A little bit. The other day, he explained some kind of dinosaur to me in great detail. We hope it's the start of something good, but we have to keep him in therapy or we might lose it. And he still can't ride in cars without anxiety…"

"Forgive me," I said. "But has he mentioned anything about the night of the shooting itself?"

Jill and Ricky glanced at each other. "No," Ricky said.

They were lying. I knew it. By the way Frankie shifted in her seat, I knew she knew it, too. And I could guess why. The kid had seen something the night of the shooting that undermined the officer's claims of innocence. And Karen had found out about it. But why did she want the kid dead?

"Listen," I said. "Why would Karen care about Anthony? Or this case?"

"No idea," Jill said, shaking her head. "I mean, she wasn't involved in any way, except maybe she was one of the officials who we talked to at some point? Before they decided not to prosecute the officer. I can't remember. That whole time in my life…"

Jill trailed off, staring deep into her garden's rough weeds. This was going nowhere. I debated coming clean and telling them what Karen wanted with their boy, but something told me that was a bad idea. We had several hours until we were supposed to meet Frankie's ex-boyfriend for the killing party, which was plenty of time to figure out what to do next, without attracting an undue amount of attention from Karen or anyone else. Keeping this family calm—and not doing anything potentially stupid—might be key to figuring out how to survive this weird and terrible situation.

"But earlier, you told us that Karen's involvement was 'ironic,'" Frankie said. "And you laughed. What did you mean by that?"

"Just that, well, she's a prosecutor, right? She's not supposed to be covering anything up." Jill locked eyes with us, more in control. "Definitely she had no connection to Bruce Melinek, the officer who they say shot my eldest son."

She was fully armored up. Or was she trying to tell us something, but too scared of what might happen?

"Okay." Frankie stood, gesturing for me to do the same. "Thank you for your time. And sorry to barge in on you like this. We only want to figure out what's going on."

"Here, take my number." Jill levered in her seat so she could pry her phone from her jeans. "Ready?"

Frankie typed her number into her phone's contacts app as Jill rattled off the digits. "Thank you."

"You're welcome." Jill peered at me, evaluating. It made me nervous. I turned to follow Frankie, who was already headed for the garden gate, and saw a little boy crouched behind a small forest of dead plants on the back porch, watching us. I recognized him from the photos we'd uncovered online: Anthony.

I waved, and he waved back. And offered a sweet, gap-toothed smile.

I wondered what he knew.

19

Back in the car, I tapped on my phone's news app and typed in search terms ("fire," "Idaho," "murder") that might surface any article about our recent adventures up north. I was about to give up when a headline and link popped up, less a story than a quick dispatch from a local blog: fire, fatalities, unknown dead, police already on scene.

I showed the screen to Frankie. "Not good," she said.

"No. But no way could the cops keep a lid on it long. Not after that whole town burned."

While Baker and his shitbag friends had pursued us through the woods, we had stumbled upon an old mining town, long abandoned. Along its main street, we found the world's creepiest hotel, which we used as an ambush site to kill some of our pursuers, including Rob, my neighbor. In the course of that gunfight, we set parts of the town on fire, and I assumed that, given the remoteness of the location and the lack of a local fire department, every building would burn to ash.

None of that bothered me, but I would feel pretty bad if the inferno chewed up a couple hundred acres of wilderness. It had been a dry year, with forest fires shredding parts of Idaho and Oregon every few weeks, and I had zero desire to put any fire-fighters or civilians in danger. Although Idaho authorities were very good about shutting down roads and posting evacuation notices, shifting winds could put an RV park or a campground

115

at risk before anyone realized what was happening.

I had to keep those thoughts away for the time being. "Like you said in the car last night, it'll take them a long time to get a full forensics team out there," I said. "And we took all their wallets and phones. They'll have a hard time figuring out the identities of the bodies, never mind what actually happened." Especially since many of those bodies were splattered in little pieces all over the woods, providing a couple hundred bite-sized snacks for coyotes and bears.

"Unless Karen leaks something to them."

"She's going to hold off. Like you said, we're potentially valuable to her."

"I hope so, bro." Starting the SUV's engine, she glanced at the house we'd exited. "What'd you think?"

"I think those parents definitely know something, and no way they'll tell two random strangers who show up at their door. Faking like we were journalists was a good idea, but not good enough."

"Solution?"

"I have an idea, but you're not going to like it."

"I don't like anything that's been going on, so what's one more bit of crap?"

"I call one of my cop friends, I get him to talk about the shooting. Maybe he'll provide some detail that lets us tie everything together."

Frankie pulled from the space and accelerated hard down the street. "That's not very smart."

"Walk me through your thinking, O Great One."

"Karen's brother—one of the richest and most powerful men in the state—is killed in a freak accident, and then you show up a day later asking about some case that Karen was involved in? Cops aren't stupid. He'll figure something is up."

"Maybe not. We're not supposed to know anything about what happened up north. There's nothing connecting us. He'll assume coincidence."

"That's not how cops think. They can't help themselves. Everything's potentially connected to something else."

"I think it's worth the risk. What other options do we have?"

"Right now, running to Mexico is seeming like a better and better option."

"Then we're in agreement." I grinned. "I'm calling my friend."

Frankie sighed. "You better be careful. Hungry?"

I was starving again, I realized. Or maybe my hunger had never fully disappeared. My body craved not only fuel, but the comfort of carbohydrates, sugar, alcohol. "Heck yes," I said.

Frankie veered left, hard, into the drive-thru lane of a local establishment that served some of the best milkshakes, sundaes, and burgers in the Treasure Valley. As she ordered two extra-large chocolate milkshakes, two double-cheeseburgers with bacon, and an epic bag of fries, I dialed Harry. The call went straight to voicemail, and I left a message for him to call me back as soon as he could.

After we retrieved our food from the drive-thru window, Frankie maneuvered us back onto the street, then took a quick right into a convenient alley. She parked in the shade of an apartment building, killed the engine, and handed over my grease-sodden bag of calories.

"Thank you," I said, tearing open the moist paper and fishing out the cheeseburger and wolfing down half of it in three bites. I barely finished chewing when my phone rang: Harry calling me back.

I answered it. "Yeah?"

"Jake?"

It wasn't Harry. "Who is this?" I asked.

"It's Bob, Harry's partner. What, you don't know the lovely sound of my voice?"

"What are you doing with Harry's phone?"

"He's temporarily indisposed. Can I help you with something?"

"I need to speak to Harry. It's important."

"We're downtown. Swing on by." He gave me the address.

I hung up. Frankie stared at me silently, her eyebrow cocked. "Obviously I'm not going with you," she said.

"No, you are not."

"Where are you meeting?"

I told her.

"Okay. I am going to *lurk* nearby, and you're going to call me the second you're done, okay? Or if you're in trouble."

"Okay."

"And don't you dare say anything stupid."

"Oh, come on." I threw a fry at her. "I'm not some kind of mouth-breathing moron, sis."

She smirked. "Could have fooled me."

20

On the short drive to my meeting with the cops, Frankie flicked on the radio, which promptly offered us the worst possible update: Very Important People had been killed under mysterious circumstances, and law enforcement was investigating as fast and thoroughly as it could. I knew Frankie's very capable men had scrubbed the scene thoroughly, wiping fingerprints from scorched metal and collecting all phones and identification cards—but what if they had missed something?

The Idaho weather (and the animals) would degrade DNA evidence, making a nightmare out of most forensics, but what I'd learned from my years of bounty hunting was that criminals had a tendency to miss enough little things to send them to jail for life. A photograph snapped by a traffic camera, for example, or a stray hair stuck in a drain.

"Janine would totally love Mexico," Frankie said. "Nice beaches, great food. What's not to like?"

"Let's just deal with this."

We headed downtown along 9th Street. On the corner of Bannock, we passed a cute cider bar, its outdoor seating loaded with hipsters. A long time ago, that same building housed the bar where I had my unfortunate encounter with Stevie, Hanzo Sandman, and the Cab of the Future. I had thought my life hit rock bottom that day, but I'd been deluding myself. It can always get worse. After the nuclear bombs fall, when the last surviving human takes refuge in a murder bunker far beneath the earth, they're going to assume that life has achieved Peak Awful—until they realize that the bunker is stocked only with raspberry-flavored protein bars and the complete discography of Celine Dion.

Frankie pulled over a block beyond the cider bar. "I trust you got this, bro," she said, squeezing my shoulder. "I am going to be a block away, doing my best to watch, and if you smell anything—and I mean the very faintest whiff of shit—you phone me and I'll come running, you hear?"

"I got it."

"I know you do, but you better do it. I know you have this pesky love of law and order—as if somehow that shit is going to love you back—but if it comes down to you and a cop, you better believe I'm going to blast that cop's brains all over the nearest wall."

"Thanks for the mental image."

"You can handle it."

"But I'm going to borrow this," I said, opening the glove compartment and removing her pistol. Without waiting for her to agree, I exited the vehicle, opened the trunk, and removed the windbreaker. The fabric was faded, the elbows worn down, but I wasn't trying to make a fashion statement: I just needed a way to hide the pistol, which I shoved down the back of my jeans.

Bob wanted to meet in a pizza place famous for its quality. I knew it well, having stopped there many nights for a slice or three on my way home. I found the stencils of the New York skyline on the wall charming, although I often ordered my pizza to go rather than dealing with the rowdy teenagers who filled the tables after school.

For my purposes today, here was the best part: past the bathrooms, an unmarked door led into the adjoining office building, which (if memory served) offered a number of exits. Plenty of escape routes if something went weird, which, knowing how my day went, it probably would.

Bob and Harry sat at a table to the left of the counter, plates with half-eaten slices in front of them. Bob had a large white bandage on the left side of his head, an inch above the ear. Both cops had their backs to the wall, which would place my back to the door if I took the seat in front of them. Not acceptable. As I walked toward them, I picked up a chair and dragged it against the wall to Bob's left, so all three of us would face the door.

I took my seat. "It's more comfortable this way," I told them. I kept one hand in my lap, while the other I dangled along the side of the chair. I would only need a fraction of a second to slip it under the windbreaker and pull the pistol.

After a long pause, Bob stood and moved his chair, placing his back to the front door. "Good to see you again," Harry said. "All of your guns in working order, I take it?"

"They were indeed," I said. "Thank you."

"What can we do for you?" Bob asked. "We're on a schedule here."

"Did either of you fine gents work the Ewan McKee case?"

They tensed. Bob glanced around the restaurant. Aside from the pimply kid working the counter, and another teenager at the table beside the front windows, the place was empty. The radio atop the soda cooler blared a pop hit that would drown out our conversation, provided we kept our voices low enough. The teenager at the front table also wore a pair of wireless headphones and was staring at a tablet, which meant we could set off a bomb in here without him noticing.

"I assume at least one of you did," I said, "based on how you're acting."

"Why do you want to know about that?" Harry asked.

"I got a bounty," I said. "Relative says that the guy used to hang out with Ewan as a kid."

"Really," Bob said. "What was this gentleman's name?"

"Eddy Morris," I said. That was a lie, but I would be long gone by the time they had the opportunity to run the database for a hit.

"It was a real stain on this department," Harry offered. "Now, you hear a lot of bullshit about how it was a targeted killing. How the officer did it on purpose. I don't think that for a second. Any traffic stop is an opportunity for things to go wrong. Your blood is up, you're tired if you've been working a long shift..."

"It was a mistake," Bob snapped. "A dumb accident. Everyone felt bad about it, but the past is the past."

"What happened to your head, Bob?" I asked.

"Car accident," he replied, feeling the edges of the bandage. "Not in the line of duty. Doc says it'll heal in a week."

"That's too bad."

"Yes. Sorry we couldn't be more helpful. Is there anything else we might assist with? Because in case you haven't heard, we got a real bad situation brewing up north."

"That's what Harry told me the other night," I said. "The news said a lot of people died up there?"

"Not just any people." Bob sighed. "I'll miss that guy's radio program."

"What?" I asked, although I knew he was referring to John the Barbarian, the ultra-wealthy shock jock who had participated in the Boise Longpig Hunting Club, and who paid for his sins when my wife and sister beat him to death with a rock.

"Never mind. Bunch of rich folks, that's who died," Bob said. "Which makes it the biggest red ball this department's ever gotten. So big that everyone's working on it, even if it's not technically our jurisdiction."

"I'm sorry to hear that," I said. "I'd ask which rich people, but I don't know anybody rich."

"Somehow I doubt that," Bob said, offering me a significant look.

"The officer who shot that kid, is that why he suffered no consequences? Because it was an accident?" I took a deep breath with lungs that suddenly felt too tight. "Or did Karen have something to do with it?"

Harry twisted his head. "Karen who?"

"Karen Baker," I said.

"The prosecutor?" Bob said. "I worked with her a few times. Got no idea what she'd have to do with the McKee case. Are you saying she might have pulled some strings?"

Wonderful: another dead end. "I don't know what I'm asking," I said, trying to power forward. "You know any bad actors that McKee was associated with? Any clues that would help me find this guy?"

"What did you want, ah, this Eddy Morris for?" Harry asked.

"Car theft."

"Nah, I'm drawing a blank, but maybe we can run it through the system," Bob said.

"You have any information for us?" Harry shoved his last bit of pizza in his mouth, chewed. "About that whole up-north situation?"

"None," I said. "I've been taking some me-time lately. Thinking of getting into another line of work, in fact."

Bob chuckled. "What's that? Running guns like your sister?"

"Maybe I'll rejoin the military. Go back to the Middle East. It'll be more relaxing."

"Anyway." Harry stood, gesturing for Bob to follow. "We got to run. Let me know if you want us to run that Eddy Morris guy."

"Will do." Anxious to get out of here, I stood and headed for the rear door. I planned to slip through the office building beyond, out the nearest exit, and walk in a random pattern through downtown until I was sure no cops were following me. Only then would I find Frankie, and we could flee.

To my surprise, Bob immediately began to follow me, not the least bit subtle about it. Behind him, Harry's mouth opened, as if he was about to say something, before he jogged to catch up with Bob.

I held the rear door open for Bob. "Didn't realize you were going this way."

123

He shrugged, not quite meeting my eyes. That was weird, too. Turning away from him, I proceeded toward the brightly lit exit sign at the end of this long, grayly carpeted hallway. If this was some kind of weird intimidation tactic, it wasn't going to work. I would walk until both of these cops passed out from exhaustion. Given Harry's cigar habit, that would probably take a grand total of thirty minutes.

"Get in the elevator," Bob said.

I looked at his face, then his hands. In the transition from pizza parlor to hallway, while I was fumbling with the door, he had drawn a small pistol from somewhere on his person. Not his service weapon; it was a Kahr P380, a very small and expensive gun. His slight-of-hand was actually impressive: I liked to think of myself as someone always hyper-aware of his environment, but Bob had skills I'd never considered.

"What is that?" I said.

"Move," Bob replied, and jabbed the gun into my ribs.

"Or what, you're going to shoot me?" I jutted my chin at the door. "Ten feet from a bunch of kids in there? What's going on here?"

"Yeah, Bob?" Harry's voice trembled. "Are we arresting him? On what grounds?"

"Let's go in the elevator," Bob said. "Hit the button."

I did, hoping that, when the doors opened, a bunch of office workers—witnesses—would spill out. What the hell did Bob want? Harry clearly had no idea what was going on.

When the elevator doors opened, the car was empty. I stepped onboard and immediately pivoted, pushing myself against the wall, my hands crossed behind my back. Bob hadn't patted me down, the idiot. I could feel the heavy outline of Frankie's pistol against my thumbs. Bob had the drop on me, sure, but that could change in an instant. I just needed a distraction.

Harry stepped into the car behind Bob, sounding worried: "What are we doing here?"

"It's okay, partner," Bob said, a little too rushed and loud. A single bead of sweat rolled down his brow. "I'll explain every-thing. We have a dangerous criminal here. Hit the button for the roof, would you?"

Harry obeyed. That's the thing about cops. You followed your partner's orders on reflex, because to do otherwise might mean death for both of you. A similar principle held in the Ar-my: you ducked when someone shouted a warning, at least if you wanted your head to stay on your body.

The doors shut, and the elevator rose. "Bob, you tell me what's going on," Harry said. "Right now."

"That bad shit happening up north?" Bob said. "It's all Jake's fault."

"Wait, what? How do you know?" Harry asked. "Shouldn't we bring him in for questioning?"

"You know, you're right." Bob turned toward him. "Let's cuff him. I'll explain on the way back to the station."

Harry smiled as he reached for the handcuffs on his belt. They were back in the land of normalcy. "Why don't you explain no..."

He never finished his sentence before Bob shot him in the eye.

21

Harry dropped like a puppet with its strings severed, leaving most of his head splattered on the wall behind him. Bob began to swing the smoking pistol in my direction, but he should have let Harry cuff me before blowing his brains out. I grabbed Bob's wrist and twisted as hard as I could, forcing him to drop the weapon.

Bob swung his other fist at my chin, but I was faster. I slammed a foot into the back of his knee, dropping him with a groan, and, gripping the back of his skull, rammed his face into the side of the elevator as hard as I could. Although I had no special love for Harry, killing a cop in my presence was more shit I didn't need this week.

Wheezing through a busted nose, Bob made the mistake of trying to lunge for his dropped pistol, so I stomped on his fingers, which broke with a meaty crunch. The elevator stopped at the roof, the doors opening to reveal a short corridor ending in a pair of double doors. A burst of fresh air swept into the car, pushing back the coppery stench of blood.

"Let's go," I said, yanking the elevator's emergency stop button to keep it in place. If they had a maintenance person on-site, we might only have a few minutes before they showed up, but I planned on leaving long before then. My other concern was any-one on the rooftop itself. I liked my odds on that front, though.

With Bob's collar in one hand and Bob's pistol in the other, I dragged him out of the elevator. His scrambling feet smeared Harry's blood, leaving a rough trail behind us. "We're going to have us a little chat," I said as I shouldered open the double doors, leading us onto the flat rooftop blessedly empty of people. Boise is a low-rise city, and I felt reasonably certain that nobody in the office buildings in the distance would notice us.

"Can't...kill...me..." Bob wheezed. "I'm...cop."

"More like cop killer." Tossing the pistol to my right, I dragged him over to the small concrete shred to our left. "Lean against that."

He did, and I patted him down, stripping away badge and handcuffs and throwing them toward the discarded pistol. Next, I pocketed his phone, figuring it might come in useful at some point. "Now," I said. "You just killed your partner. Why is that?"

"Your...fault..."

"Wrong answer." I hit him in the head bandage, lightly, and he winced in pain. My adrenaline was draining away, allowing me to think more clearly. I should have restrained him with his own handcuffs. Hopefully he was too hurt to try anything stupid. "Once again, for the daily bonus: why?"

"Karen." He spat blood and snorted. When he spoke again, his voice was a little clearer, but he wheezed out his nostrils like an excited buffalo. "When you said her name...and that McKee kid...you signed Harry's death warrant."

"Why? How do you know Karen?" I examined the bandage. "Were you at my house the other night?"

"Your fucking sister." He flashed bloody teeth. "Knocked me out."

"You're lucky she didn't kill you. Harry didn't know what you were doing?"

Bob shook his head.

We were running short of time. "Karen," I said. "Tell me everything. Go."

"No. They'll...kill me."

"Fucker, I'll kill you," Frankie said behind me. "Better share with the class."

I spun, too surprised to say anything. My sister stood silhouetted by the sun, her sunglasses transforming her eye sockets into black pits, and although she barely came up to my chest in boots, she nonetheless seemed to loom, transformed into the angel of death that her rivals whispered about in the slow hours of the night. She walked toward us, and Bob pressed his back against the side of the shed as if the concrete would magically let him through.

"This is Bob," I said. "Harry's partner. Harry's the dead one in there."

"Bob kill him? Or did you?"

"Bob. We were about to discuss why."

Frankie invaded Bob's airspace, towering over him, her hands balled into fists. "I'm so curious. Bro, you break his nose?"

Before I could answer, Bob nodded vigorously.

"Oh, I recognize this dude." Frankie knelt beside him, her left hand in her pocket. She drew out a small nub of pencil, holding it so Bob could see. "We meet again. I'm sorry about knocking you cold the other night, so I want to make it up to you. I'm going to fix your nose, okay?"

Bob stared cross-eyed at the pencil. "What?"

"Hold very still." While her right hand clenched his scalp, her left slipped the pencil slowly up his left nostril. Bob whined, his eyes rolling toward me for any sign of support or salvation. Frankie clucked her tongue twice, and when Bob looked back at her, she pushed his head sharply to the right with the pencil still angled upward. We heard the cereal crunch of Bob's nose resetting.

Bob's eyes went very wide, and he howled. Frankie yanked the pencil loose, and a spray of blood poured out the nostril and decorated Bob's chin and collar. When Bob took a deep breath for a fresh scream, the air whistled up his noise quiet and clear. And when he spoke, his voice was almost normal again, only a little bubbly from the blood in his throat.

"Oh shit," he said, looking at Frankie with something like wonder.

"Trust me, it's easier to do on yourself than someone else." With the red-smeared pencil, she pointed at her own nose with its prominent bump, an artifact of no fewer than four or five breaks over the years. "Sort of like tying a tie."

Bob bent and carefully spat blood to his right, away from Frankie. "I'll tell you," he said, "but you got to let me off this roof, okay? I shot my partner, and I need to live with that for the rest of my life, but I swear, I'll cover it up."

"Karen," Frankie said. "Now."

"Okay, okay. Have you ever heard of Keith Baker?"

"Sure," I said. "Karen's nephew. He's a serious addict. Before that, he was a cop. Did you know him?"

"Oh yeah," Bob sighed. "Everyone knew Keith. Total asshole. He had a drug habit back then, too, that he barely kept under control. We all covered for him, because of his family, but we shouldn't have. If I had to do it all over again, I'd never have told him when the piss tests were coming up."

"He got kicked off the force," Karen said. "Drugs?"

Bob shook his head. "The McKee kid. Keith was the one who shot him."

"No," I said. "There was another name in all the news reports. Some other officer."

"Yeah, Keith's partner. He agreed to take the fall, in exchange for a big payout. But it was Keith who made the stop, approached the car. I guess he was high off his ass because he thought the McKee kid had a gun, shot him. And that wasn't the worst part."

"What was that?" I wanted to hear all of this, but I knew we were short of time. As soon as someone headed up here to reset the elevator, our problems would multiply.

"Keith started shouting all kinds of racist shit. Who knows what was going on in his head? Cruiser's dashboard camera captured every word. Plus, they told me that Ewan's little brother started speaking again, just recently. He said the word

'Keith' in therapy."

"According to the news, the dashboard camera was corrupted," I said. "I guess that was a lie, right?"

"It was deleted." Bob shrugged. "But there are copies. Like on my phone. Which is another reason you can't kill me, because I got a copy of it on there, and the phone's locked..."

Poor Bob, he looked almost hopeful as he said it. As if he didn't know my sister's reputation for putting heads on pikes.

Frankie's expression was almost tender. "You work for Karen?"

"Yes. And Harry didn't," Bob said. "Sooner or later, he would have put the pieces together. If only you hadn't come around with your questions, he'd still be alive...if only..."

Frankie held out a hand. "Bro, give me his phone."

"It's on there, believe me," Bob said. "Right in the videos and photos. It's my insurance policy, too. And only I know my passcode..."

I handed over the phone. Frankie took it, and, rattler-quick, snatched Bob's broken fingers. Bob shrieked in surprise and pain as she pressed his thumb against the glass, unlocking the device. "Biometrics, they're so secure." Frankie grinned in Bob's face as she gave the phone back to me. "Bro, keep playing with the screen. Make sure it doesn't go back to sleep and lock."

Bob's eyes widened. "What?"

"It's a sad story." Frankie stood, her knees crackling. "You shot your partner, then you were so upset over what you did, you came up here and threw yourself off the roof. Who knows why? Cops, sometimes they lose their minds."

I moved away from them, tapping open every app on the phone. I knew what was coming next, and while under different circumstances I might have tried to stop my sister, I couldn't forget that Bob had tried to murder me. I was fresh out of sympathy today.

Frankie gripped Bob's collar, yanking him upright. "Bro," she said. "Bob shot Harry with that pistol on the roof there?"

"That's right."

"You touch it?"

"Yeah. I'll wipe it."

"Okay. Don't forget to keep that phone awake."

Bob was blubbering. "Please, we can talk about this, can't we? Can't..."

"You were going to kill my brother, so, um, no."

They were nearly to the edge of the roof, and Bob decided that he might as well go down fighting. He drove an elbow backward, aiming for Frankie's ribs, but he was sloppy and slow, and she sidestepped it easily. Before he could spin around, she lashed a foot into his right ankle, dropping him to his knees; and as he scrambled for balance, his arms pinwheeling, she kicked him in the back, sending him into the void headfirst. A quick scream, a wet impact.

"Nothing but net," Frankie said, trotting past me. "Keep that phone on."

I finished wiping the pistol with the hem of my shirt, then ran after her. We had two or three minutes at most before the first police arrived. Plenty of time to reach the ground floor, then duck through one of the fire exits. I felt bad about Harry's useless death. Another body to add to Karen's tab.

22

Bob's phone had nearly a full charge. As we ducked into Frankie's SUV and Frankie drove us a few blocks north, away from the growing chaos surrounding the pile of meat formerly known as Bob, I sifted through Bob's videos—there were a suspicious number of clips from Korean music videos, young girls writhing in miniskirts under flashing lights—until I found one with no thumbnail image, labeled "VID_528491."

Tapping it open, I tilted the phone so Frankie could better see the screen. It was indeed dashboard-cam footage, grainy and overexposed, with the sound muffled to the point of distortion. We saw an officer—clean-shaven, in uniform, but recognizably Keith—glance once through the windshield, at the camera, before walking toward the driver's side of a dark Toyota pulled to the curb, a lit flashlight in his hand. Keith's partner paralleled him on the opposite side of the car, but the angle and shadows made it impossible to see a face.

Keith swept his flashlight into the Toyota's rear seat before proceeding to the driver's window. I couldn't see either McKee boy inside the vehicle. Keith bent, chatting with the driver. A flicker as a hand extended from the window, holding a white blur that I assumed was a driver's license and registration.

Something went wrong. Keith scrambled back, hand slapping at his belt, pistol in his hand, and then he was firing into the car, not one or two shots but the entire clip. His firearm emptied, he reloaded and fired again, three blooms of fire at almost point-blank range. The Toyota's rear window blew out. Ewan McKee was surely dead by this point, and it was a miracle that a stray bullet didn't kill his younger brother. Through the windshield, the dashboard camera's terrible microphones recorded the gunshots as tinny pops.

Keith's partner, his own firearm drawn, ducked to avoid a spray of broken glass. He rose, ready to fire, but Keith had already dropped his weapon and turned away, hands waving in the air, spewing confused gibberish at the moon.

Frankie paused the video. "Well, that was some weird shit." Taking the phone from my hands, she proceeded to message and email the clip to multiple addresses. "There. We have some good insurance."

"What now?"

"We go back to the house. Probably a good idea to switch houses, actually. Then we contact Karen, tell her to shove her job offer up her ass, no way we're killing a kid."

"Think she'll buy it?"

"She'll have no choice. Whatever plans she has—running for office, inventing the longer-lasting lightbulb, whatever—she can't afford for the world to know she covered up her nephew killing a kid at a traffic stop."

I wondered why Keith had opened fire. If Bob had told the truth before Frankie sent him on a one-way ticket to the sidewalk, multiple officers must have covered for his drug habit—which was strange, since the last thing most sane cops wanted was an addict watching their backs. He must have been high during that stop, freaked out, and ended a life. It didn't take much to imagine Karen disappearing Keith's blood tests.

How many cops like Bob were on Karen's payroll? He couldn't have been the only one.

Frankie was typing something on her phone. "What are you doing?" I asked, more out of curiosity than alarm.

"Remember that email address Karen was using, the one that

sent us the info on the kid?"

"Yeah?"

"I'm sending the video to it."

I punched the dashboard, almost screaming: "Why in the holy hell would you do that?"

She shrugged. "How else are we supposed to contact them?"

She had a point.

Tapping the screen, she tossed the phone into the center console and said: "Bombs away."

My stomach dropped like when the mortar alarms started wailing on base, the voice over the speakers screaming *Incoming, Incoming, Incoming*. Panic attack, round two. Quick, bend over. Breathe deep. You're okay. You got this. Stop clenching your knees so hard. A loud ringing in my head. No. From the phone.

"Unknown number," Frankie said. "That was quick." Fishing the phone from its slot, she tapped the speaker button so we both could hear. It was Karen, her voice crackling, as if she was calling from the surface of Mars.

"Frankie," she said.

"Karen, how goes it? So great to hear from you."

"Don't try sarcasm with me, you little bitch. I'm in no mood."

"I can sense that. What can I do for you on this finest of days?"

"You broke our agreement."

"Technically, we still have some time before killing this kid. But you know what? This whole killing-a-kid thing? Didn't sit right with me."

"Well, if you're not going to respect our agreement, then I'm afraid I have no choice but to involve law enforcement."

"You're not going to ask how we got that little item we just sent?"

The line popped and hissed, Karen refusing to fill the silence.

"Let me help you," Frankie said. "It's spelled 'B-O-B.' He worked for you, right?"

A deep sigh. "I assume you're using the past tense for a good reason."

"Bob's no longer with us. He shot his partner and fell off a roof."

"Is that true?"

"Sure, it's probably on the news by now. Check your browser. I'll wait."

Another pause. When Karen came back on the line, she sounded more cautious. "Did you do something to Bob?"

"Me? Why, no. I told you, he shot his partner and jumped off a roof. Really terrible thing. I imagine there were a lot of witnesses."

"He wasn't the only cop around," Karen said. "I'm sure every single officer in this state would be very interested in what you've been up to."

"Maybe. They'd also be really interested in that video."

"Bob gave you this video?"

"Before he jumped off the roof, yeah. Said he couldn't live with himself anymore."

"What do you want?"

"You leave our family alone. In return, I make sure this video never ends up in the hands of the media or anyone else who might be interested in it."

"How do I know you'll hold up your end of this 'bargain'? Especially since you broke your word last time?"

"You don't. But you also don't have a choice. As your brother found out, I'm very hard to kill, and this video is very easy to send after I'm dead."

Karen fell silent yet again, and I allowed myself to hope—crazy as it was—that maybe she would bend. We weren't offering a bad deal, after all. Frankie could continue her highly profitable gunrunning; I could happily return to handcuffing scumbags for a miserable per hour; and Karen could have a merry time running her dead brother's fried chicken empire or whatever rich people did.

Then Karen started laughing, and I knew this whole situation was about to go straight to hell, do not pass Go, do not collect two hundred dollars.

"What if I told you to go screw yourself?" Karen said, once she caught her breath.

Frankie winced. "Excuse me?"

"Jake's wife, her name is Janine, right? Do you like your sister-in-law?"

Incoming, Incoming, Incoming. "The fuck," I whispered.

If Karen heard me, she never mentioned it. "Your men were good, Frankie, but not good enough," she said, chuckling. "That's the thing about money, dear. It buys the best people. Top notch."

Frankie gripped the edge of the steering wheel. "You fucking bitch."

"You must have really thought we're stupid. When you told them that you'd all meet at nine tonight, to do what I asked? They knew you were stalling. I knew it, too. So I decided to adjust everyone's timetable a bit."

"You miserable fuck!"

Karen laughed harder. She was in control now, her hook deep in my sister's flesh. "Language, Frankie, language. Now let me offer you a better deal. You drive out to your little safe house in Oregon, and you sit down with my representative and have a real conversation. You'll give him your phone, and my people will delete the video from your email and whatever other accounts they can find. And if we do that, Janine gets to live, and so do you. How does that sound?"

"When?"

"Um, right now."

I reached for the phone, ready to scream at Karen, threaten to rip her head clean off if she so much as put a finger on my wife. I would do it, too. If it came down to putting another set of bodies in the ground and saving my family, I would happily stick heads on pikes all day.

Frankie yanked the phone away from me, her other hand on my chest. "You be there, too," my sister said, her face pale and cold.

"No," Karen said. "No way I put myself in harm's way like that."

"Maybe I didn't fully explain myself," Frankie said, her voice calm in a way that might have frightened me deeply if I wasn't burning with my own rage. "You're going to be there, otherwise I'm going to kill your nephew, Keith. And not only am I going to kill him, but I'm going to make sure it's in the most horrible way you can imagine."

"You do that," Karen said, "and we'll kill Janine as harshly."

"And then we start killing the rest of your family. I will tie their fucking limbs to four cars and pull them apart slowly while I make you watch. On the other hand, if you've really hired the best people, they'll protect you during a meet. We can have a good old-fashioned trade-off, and everyone can go home happy. Does that work for you?"

When I was deployed overseas, many missions involved escorting one of our commanders to a meeting with a village elder. Sometimes I helped with perimeter lockdown while the old men sat inside a building, drinking tea and trading lies in stilted translation. Every so often, I was part of the main entourage, and I had the opportunity to hear some elder, via the translator, talk about centuries-long blood feuds. How they had gone to war with some tribe or family whose great-great-granddaddy had shot their great-great-granduncle and kidnapped their great-grandmother, or shit like that.

At the time, I always thought: good thing that doesn't really happen in America. That our lives aren't dominated by these multigenerational conflicts that never fucking stop. But who was I kidding? We were locked in a battle with a rich family that started out angry at us because our daddy messed up their drug deal a couple of decades ago, and now my sister was promising to kill their next generation if they kept messing with us.

"Fine," Karen said, snapping me out of my thoughts. "This evening, at seven, at your safe house."

"Okay. And one other thing."

137

"What?"

"Proof of life for Janine."

"I'll message it to you in a minute."

"Goodbye." Frankie hung up.

My hands had gone numb. I looked down and saw them clenched into hard fists, my knuckles almost popping through my skin. My stomach roiling, the acid crawling up my throat. When was the last time I felt like this? Even in Iraq, I had never approached this kind of whole-body anger, because when things descended to hell and my friends died and I spent nights picking bits of shrapnel out of my throbbing flesh, it was always just business, with my family safe a few thousand miles away.

I forced my hands open, flexing my fingers until they tingled with fresh blood. "They're going to kill us."

"Oh yeah. And they know we know that, so this is going to get tricky."

"Your men at the house…" Before we left for Boise, two trucks' worth of Frankie's men had arrived to guard the perimeter. The Monkey Man had left on an unknown errand in Boise, and I hoped he was safe. If he was alive, we needed his special brand of psychosis right now.

I knew she was feeling their deaths, despite the blankness of her expression. "They knew what was up. That's the life." She raised the phone. "That's the life."

Flicking through her contacts list, she tapped a number, then held the device to her ear. To whomever answered, she said: "Yeah, it's me. Take care of our little problem in the cabin. Make it painful but make it quick. Bring me a souvenir. Then get down to the Oregon location. Fast."

Chattering from the other end of the line.

"I don't care what souvenir," Frankie said. "It's not like I'm going to eat the fucking thing. Make sure it's bagged up tight, okay? Last time you did this, it leaked."

More chatter.

"No, I have no idea. Beware an ambush if you take the

front." She ended the call.

The blood feud would keep rolling. I breathed deep into my torso, willing my body to slow to a manageable speed. I kept thinking about how, a mere two weeks ago, everything in my life had seemed fine, perhaps a little boring. How had it all gone so wrong, so quickly?

The phone beeped. An incoming message, a small video file. I clenched my seatbelt and nodded for Frankie to tap it open.

Janine sat on our bed in Frankie's safe house, holding a phone with its screen pointed toward the camera. On that screen, a news website with the hour's murder-and-mayhem headlines. "I'm alive," she announced. "But you better get here and kill these motherfu…"

The video cut to black.

"Got to tell you, I like your wife more and more with each passing year," Frankie said, hitting the play button again. Midway through, she paused the video and pinched to zoom into the upper-right corner of the screen, centering on the mirror above the bureau. At that magnification, the world was pixelated to the verge of incoherence, but a cluster of dark brown and lighter tan dots seemed exactly like Boz's snakeskin jacket, and the dark circles behind it could have been at least five heads.

"Okay," Frankie said, more to herself than to me, and started the SUV. "Looks like we're stuck with the weapons in the back. I wish I could promise you this will turn out fine, but you know I'd be lying."

"I know."

"Just so we're clear. We got a real rattlesnake rodeo on our hands."

PART 3
BURN

23

We raced for the Oregon border, not saying anything to one another. We aimed for US 30 and the four-lane bridge that crossed over the Snake maybe ten miles south of the safe house. In the distance, beyond the river's black flow, shimmered the yellow lights of Ontario, a small town with a few gas stations and fast-food joints along its main drag. If we set off a small war, would they hear?

Every time headlights blazed in the oncoming lane, I wondered if it was the police hunting for us. I wasn't afraid of an honest one pulling us over for speeding—Frankie's fake driver's license would trigger no alarms—but I feared an officer on Karen's payroll alerted to our presence.

As we bumped over the bridge and into Oregon's inky darkness, I allowed myself to feel a little bit of hope. Sure, our chances of dying were high, but my sister and I were capable. We were angry and sore and tired and hungry, but we were capable. The only question was whether we were capable enough.

"What's the plan?" I asked.

"Remember that back way I mentioned? Through the valley?"

"Yeah?"

"We'll go through there. Take this party directly up the butt. Sound good?"

"Never say 'directly up the butt' to me again. Are there snakes?"

"Yes, and you're wearing boots and jeans, so relax."

When I was a kid, my family would tell stories about my grandfather, a wheat farmer who died of prostate cancer a few years before I was born. As a wee lad during the Great Depression, he helped his father run bootleg liquor all over the state, earning the family quite a bit of money in the process. With that illicit cash, they bought their neighbors' land, doubling the size of the farm outside of Meridian.

Before they could use that land, they had to clear it. It's hard for anyone who grew up in a modern subdivision, surrounded by manicured lawns and air-conditioned houses and concrete, to realize the wildness of the Treasure Valley in those days. When it came to acreage, if it wasn't a field ready for planting crop, it was a tangle of chest-high grass, trees, and rocks. A perfect breeding ground for rattlesnakes.

Whenever he needed to explore the wilder edges of his holdings, my grandfather would cut a sturdy branch from a tree, maybe four or five feet long, and use it to sweep the tall grass in front of him. The way my family told the story, dozens of rattlesnakes would strike the stick before fleeing. By the time he walked a few acres, the tip of the stick had turned green with poison, shredded by fangs. It always made me shudder, imagining him stomping a path through the shimmering yellow fields, his shirt soaked in sweat, the air alive with that heart-stopping rattle.

I would have cut a firebreak around those fields and set them ablaze, let the reptiles burn. But my grandfather was made of sterner stuff—he needed to show those poisonous buggers that he ruled the land, not them.

When I moved onto my property with my family, I kept my lawns mowed and the back acreage cleared. Only a few times a year did I see a solitary rattlesnake, usually sunning itself on the driveway, and my solution was always the same: 12-gauge shotgun, buckshot, headshot. I was fine with the pellets leaving silvery streaks on the concrete, so long as I sent the creature to its Maker with a minimum of fuss. One of my friends, an excavator operator, once suggested that I follow his example and use birdshot ammo in a pistol, which he said would kill the animal without accidentally blowing a hole in anything useful, but that kind of load is only effective at ten feet or so. I've always preferred to shoot a rattlesnake from the longer-range comfort of my front doorway.

You could say I have a bit of a phobia.

"Seriously," Frankie said. "You've been a Westerner your whole life. You'd think you'd have gotten over that snake thing by now."

"Nah. I think it's one of my finer character traits, actually. My one weakness."

We laughed, and it felt good. Thinking about my wife tied to a chair somewhere, frightened, was like staring into the sun: impossible for more than a few seconds. All I wanted—so deeply that I felt it in my bones—was my normal life again, with its normal problems. Heck, was I feeling *nostalgic* about days cuffing dull scumbags, because at least that was predictable.

As we approached the turnoff to Frankie's safe house, she slowed to the legal speed. In the microsecond glimpse I had of the dirt road and the fields to either side, nothing seemed out of place. What was I expecting—a couple of men with shotguns standing in the open?

"If I had to bet, they have it blocked off near the first creek," Frankie said. "There are hills on either side, no visibility from down below, it'd be a mess."

"Your ex…"

"Yeah?"

"How many guys can he deploy?"

"'Deploy'? What are you, back in Iraq?"

"Sorry, it's the mindset I get into."

"That's the weird thing: Boz was always a low-key operator, despite how he dresses. His crew was never very big. And Karen had those rent-a-cops, but this is way too heavy for them. I have no idea who we glimpsed in that video."

"I counted five guys, based on the little smudges that might have been heads."

"Dangerous to guess like that."

"No shit."

"Let's assume fifteen guys, at least, just to be safe. Moreover, we have to assume that, after the little incident at your house, Karen went back and signed up for the premium package with whatever gunman-rental bullshit she's using."

I winced. "We can't fight fifteen guys."

"We killed almost that many a few days ago."

"Okay, sure, but those were civilians, not trained fighters."

"They weren't civilians."

"You know what I mean. Guys who've never fought anyone who shot back."

"Better. We don't kill civilians, remember? We're not like them."

"Okay."

Frankie slowed and turned off onto a dirt lane, flicking off her headlights as she did so. We drove another fifty yards before she braked gently, swerving the SUV into the ditch and behind a high tangle of prickly bushes. "It's all bushwhacking from here," she said. "Get the guns out of the back."

We had no carrying cases for the weaponry or ammunition. I could stuff the extra five-round magazine for the TAC-338 into my rear pocket, plus eight 12-gauge shells into my left hip pocket. Full loads in the guns. I hoped that was enough.

"How far is it?" I asked as I slung the sniper rifle over my shoulder. Propping the shotgun and the UMP against the rear bumper, I closed the trunk, wondering why Frankie hadn't answered—and turned to see her dim shadow walking away from me.

By the way she moved, setting her heel against her toe with every step, I knew she was counting out paces. Another one of her famous caches, no doubt. How did she remember where they were all placed? Then again, she once memorized most of the Bible word-for-word so she could torture our next-door neighbor with discussions about logically contradictory verses; keeping a couple dozen geographic coordinates in the back of her mind should have been no problem.

Kneeling down, Frankie dug with her hands. By the time I reached her, she had uncovered what looked like the top half of a gallon paint container. Prying off the lid, she drew out a black, bulky cylinder that she handed to me.

"For the rifle," she said.

It was a night-vision scope. "It's like Christmas morning," I said, flicking it on.

Nothing happened.

"Battery's dead," I said. "You got extra batteries in there? Or one of those recharger packs?"

"Got one for the phones, not for the scope." Frankie rooted around in the bucket. "Dammit, sorry. I don't know when I checked this cache last."

Hell of a mistake, I thought. "What else you got in there?"

"Zippo, traffic flares, extra phone, knife." Stuffing those items into her pants pockets, she stood. "I got to organize these buckets better. Sometimes I get a little whimsical, you know what I mean?"

"What do you mean by 'whimsical'? Did you bury a rubber chicken out there somewhere?"

"Maybe I should. Couple thousand years from now, long after we're dead and forgotten, some archeologist could dig it up, wonder what the fuck we were up to. We could confuse history studies for a generation."

"You're so weird, kid," I said, and, as Frankie led off into the night, I swung by the SUV to retrieve the guns from the bumper. Catching up to her, I handed over the UMP.

It was a shorter walk than I expected. As we started off, I checked my phone long enough to verify the total lack of signal, then turned it off. That brief second with a lit screen totally destroyed my night vision, and I needed to wait for it to return. Meanwhile I heard Frankie marching away from me, her feet crunching dry grass.

Once I could see, I tore after her. Twenty minutes later, we arrived at the edge of a steep cliff, the land falling away in a gravel waterfall sprinkled with massive boulders. At the bottom, the river glimmered silver in the quarter-moon. On the far side of the water, the cliffs rose sharply, throwing the overgrown valley into deepest shadow. Frankie's safe house wasn't visible from here, although I guessed it was roughly straight ahead of us, hidden by the cliffs' jagged crown of rocks.

We knelt so nobody would see us silhouetted against the sky. I whispered: "You've done this route in the dark?"

She pointed to our right, where the cliffs on our side leveled off into a narrow shelf of gray rock. "There's a hot spring down there that I use a lot, and a little cave."

"Okay."

"It's a pretty good sniper nest. Hey, look at that." She pointed to the far side of the valley. The human eye is very good at picking out movement, even in terrible light, and I followed her finger to a slightly blacker dot—no more than a shadow on a shadow—moving between what might have been two piles of rock. A moment later, another flicker of movement maybe twenty yards to the left.

"They're waiting for us," Frankie said, and cursed. "There's one pathway that runs up there. It's maybe ten feet at the narrowest, where there's rocks. Forty feet in the patches where it gets wide."

In other words, it didn't matter if three or three dozen guys waited for us down there: picking through that overgrown jumble of grass and rock would slow us down, and, with a cliff wall on one side and a drop to the river on the other, only two trained men with guns could keep us pinned forever.

"Head to the cave," Frankie said. "Get set up."

I had no idea how I'd find targets without a night-vision scope. "You coming with me?"

"No, you're going to have to do your own spotting."

"How am I supposed to see squat?"

Frankie stuck a finger in her mouth, then held it high above her head. "Wind's to the east."

"What?"

"I'll provide the light."

"Huh?"

"Don't be dense, just listen. Once you're in position, I'm going to cross down on our left. There's a big patch of trees by the riverbank. Goes onto this little beach." Clapping me on the shoulder, she crept away, swallowed almost instantly by the night.

24

Climbing down to the cave was easier than I thought. Centuries of boiling water from the hot spring had carved out a pocket inside the cliff big enough to stand in, if I ducked my head a little. Its rear sloped seamlessly to a floor of smooth stone, ensuring that my back was protected.

I lay flat on my stomach, unhinged the bipod legs from the rifle, and set the weapon in the center of the cave mouth. When I pulled the trigger, the gunfire would echo off the stone around me and pummel my eardrums to mush. Not that praying for ear protection would do me any good at this juncture. I set my spare magazine beside me, along with the shotgun.

A trickle of hot water ran from a crack in the rocks to my right, steaming as it filtered through the gravel. A few sandbags and big rocks stood out against the uniform grayness of the cliff, ready for Frankie and her friends to push them together and create a makeshift hot tub. Once I started shooting, folks down there would fire back, and hopefully the sandbags would serve as false targets.

I had no formal training as a sniper but when I was a kid my daddy taught me the basics of using a scope. Much later, in Mosul, a pair of bored Delta operators assigned to overwatch my platoon had talked me through wind and range and concepts like the Coriolis effect, where the curvature of the Earth can affect your longest-range shots. I had used that knowledge to kill more than a few deer over the years at what I had thought was an insane distance but now, peering through the scope at the jagged notch of the valley, I felt only fear that I would somehow mess this up.

I sent up a quick prayer to those Delta guys, wherever they were, as I tweaked my scope and made sure for the twentieth time that my safety was off. The wind was hard out of the north, strong enough to whistle over the stony lips of the cave mouth, and I kept picturing my bullets arcing wide of their targets, sparking uselessly off rock while my sister fought and died alone. I took deep breaths, trying to will that vision away.

My sister and I had torn through any number of killers and thugs over the course of our short and brutal lives, but most of those guys had been amateurs or criminals with no formal training. These were mercenaries—Karen had called them the best that money could buy—and if I wanted my whole family to live to the weekend, I needed to put aside my bone-deep aversion to hurting former soldiers.

I should have asked Frankie more about her plan. *I'll provide the light.* What did that mean? I hoped she wouldn't try to draw their fire, expecting me to sight and kill them based on their muzzle flashes. She knew that wouldn't work. What was she up to?

I was about to find out. In the scope, I found that space in the river she'd mentioned, packed with trees. A dark smudge that I assumed was Frankie emerged from the silvery water, disappeared into the underbrush, and appeared a minute later in the faint sliver of grassland beyond. From this angle I could see the vague hint of her arm outstretched. She was holding something. A gun?

A bright burst of red.

No, it was that traffic flare she had retrieved from the cache. What the hell? Did she want them to see her? With the flare's bloody light playing over her face, she looked very small against the looming darkness of the mountains and trees.

Then I remembered what she said about the wind.

"Oh, this is some bullshit," I murmured.

Holding the flare at hip level, Frankie trotted across the field, pausing every few feet to duck and set another patch of dry grass on fire. It reminded me of when we were kids, and our uncles would hire men to clear the acreage behind their farmhouse outside of Sand Hollow. Those men had a propane-fueled flamethrower to torch the tall grass, making sure to keep the wind at their backs and the fire at their fronts, and the fields would always burn far faster than I anticipated, the inferno roaring like a beast as it ate.

Stay back, the men always told us.

Get too near the flames, and you'll die. The smoke is so hot it'll crisp your lungs.

After that, I always harbored a healthy fear of fire to go along with my fear of snakes. Not Frankie, though. Having run in a circle, she tossed the flare overhand into the brush and sprinted back into the river, leaning hard against the fast current. Unslinging the rifle from her back, she lowered herself into the rushing waters up to her chest.

Up here, I already smelled faint smoke. The wind would keep most of it away from the cave, but it might hide my view downrange. I swiveled to focus on the valley as the blooming firelight glinted orange and red on the cliffs. Maybe a hundred yards from where Frankie lit the flames, a pair of solid shadows moved through a shoulder-high patch of grass, disappearing behind a jumble of rocks. My finger tensed on the trigger, but I refrained from firing. Best to let the fire do its work.

The flames crept along the valley's narrow pathway, driven by the wind and fed by underbrush. It was slow at first, and a few of its crawling fingers faded into embers and darkness, but some of those embers swarmed aloft like evil fireflies and settled on fresh patches of fuel, and new flames swirled to life. When the fire's front reached a narrower part of the trail, where the canyon wall rose into two hundred feet of sheer rock, it picked up speed, with a crackle and pop I could hear over the hum of the wind.

I worried about the fire ascending to the cliffs and threatening the safe house. I seemed to remember—or hoped I remembered—a set of furrows and sandy patches beyond the backyard that would act as a firebreak.

This is insane.

Yes, yes it was. A plan that only a psychopath like Frankie could love. But what choice did we have, with these kinds of odds?

The fire gained speed, its evil light playing on the canyon walls. More movement in the brush, paired with what might have been a yell of panic or command. Still I told myself not to pull the trigger. At this point, the gunmen in the valley might have assumed this was an ordinary fire. We wanted to maintain the element of surprise for as long as we could.

Gunshots.

I snapped the scope toward Frankie in the water. She was still, her head nearly submerged. It wasn't her. Who was firing?

Another scan of the valley. Was some mouth-breathing moron popping off shots at the fire? No sign of it.

More shots echoing off the rocks, almost gentle pops from straight ahead. The safe house.

Fuck.

Didn't matter who was shooting who. Not with Janine there. This was bad. This was so bad.

I swept to Frankie, no longer in the river, no, she was on the bank, lit from behind as she ran ahead of the flames, rushing for the safe house, because now there was no time to let the fire do its cleansing work, and—

25

—Frankie sprinted faster than I'd ever seen her before, a blur through the unburnt brush and then across smoking ash, out-flanking the fire on a widening portion of the trail, a ghost in the smoke, then disappearing again in the grass, and I hoped like I'd never hoped so fervently in my wayward life that every skill she'd ever learned—from high school track star to adult gunrunner—was ready and sharp at this moment, because this moment mattered above all others, our family's life balanced on the edge of a blade, and through the scope I saw her reappear on the path, the bright embers of the fire-front playing across her face, and then she disappeared yet again, behind a gnarled tree, and I shifted the scope to my right, further down the valley, in time to catch two men emerging onto the path, the fire lighting them full—mercenaries, yes, black ballistic vests over tight black T-shirts, black baseball caps pulled low over their eyes, black cargo pants with pistols holstered on their hips—and I centered my crosshairs between the eyes of the man on the left, the bigger one with a tattoo of a dragon or snake looping from his left sleeve, and my finger tensed on the trigger, ready to take the shot, breathe in, breathe out, but I hadn't yet squeezed out that last pound of pressure when the man fell, simultaneous with the harsh clap of a gunshot echoing off rock, and I shifted my scope to the second man raising his rifle and squeezed the trigger as another gunshot rang across the valley, bullets from two different directions hitting the man in the chest and head, a red cloud as he tumbled to the dirt, leg twitching, and Frankie emerged from behind the tree, crouching to loot the bodies of anything useful—magazines of ammunition, the bigger guy's pistol, what might have been a small knife—before standing again, glancing once in my direction with a cocked eyebrow, letting me know that both kills were definitely hers, and behind her the fire was rising, even over the rifle-shot's ringing in my ears I could hear it roaring its hunger as it gained speed, oh shit, the grass no longer catching fire so much as vaporizing into bright ash, the sand roasting black under Frankie's feet as she ran again, staying low, and with a fresh round in my chamber I tracked in front of her, anxious for targets, and one presented itself—a man stepping from behind a pile of rocks, shotgun already leveled, and I fired at his head, the bullet dipping too fast as it arced across the space, impacting where his neck met his chest, right above his tactical vest, and he tumbled with his head too loose, the boom of his shotgun firing uselessly into the night, and Frankie was already past him, bracing one foot on the rock pile as she sprung into the air, firing at something I couldn't see from this angle, raking the darkness before she hit the ground, rolling, ejecting her spent magazine and popping in a new one, and I had my rifle aimed beyond her, further along the trail, where I thought I saw something but couldn't be sure, the flames throwing frantic light along the rocks, my heart was racing too fast and I was terrible at this, not a trained sniper but I had no choice, there was a pale flash in the darkness that could have been a face, gone before I could gauge and aim properly but I fired at it anyway, hoping that if it was an attacker that the bullet might freak them out, make them make a mistake that my sister could exploit as she ran, the flames thirty feet behind her and rushing almost at her pace, the air shimmering, and I realized that she should have stayed behind the fire-front, it was moving too fast, and if she leapt off the ridge to her right she would break both her legs in the shallow river and probably drown, and above the cliffs we heard more shots, good God maybe they were blasting Janine apart up there, her and whatever was left of Frankie's men, and we needed to get up there fast, fast, fast, fast, fast, and Frankie sprinted, the trail rising and narrowing, bracketed by the cliff to the water on her right and the boulders to her left, and the darkness ahead of her shattered with points of light and the rocks around her puffed and burst, and she dove onto the trail, firing back as best she could but it wasn't enough, she was pinned down as no doubt someone flanked her through the rocks, and I centered my crosshairs on the flashes and fired back once, twice, three times, knowing the range was too great, that my chance of hitting anything was virtually nil, but maybe my shots would keep their heads down long enough for Frankie to figure something out, she had to figure something out, she always figured something out, but now Frankie was screaming, gripping her shoulder and rolling to the side, too close to the ledge, the path hellishly lit by the onrushing flames, and I fumbled for a fresh magazine but I was too late, and I knew that we had lost, we lost, I'm so sorry Janine, I'm so sorry we fucked up when it mattered—

26

Fuck that.

27

I fired the extra box magazine of .338 at the muzzle flashes, then set the empty sniper rifle aside. I had no clear plan in mind, no thoughts except that I was useless up here. Without the scope, Frankie was reduced to a dark smudge on the trail, her right arm twitching as she tried to dig something from the pocket of her pants. I couldn't see anyone approaching her, and I hoped with all my heart that the flames would make her attackers cautious for another minute.

Retrieving the shotgun, I slung its strap around my back and exited the cave at a run, not letting myself think about the stupidity of sliding down the steep cliffside even as I did it. I kept my legs pointed downslope and somewhat loose, and, twisting my body, jammed my left hand into the scree as a rough brake, and in that painful position I slid down the incline, faster and faster, the blurred river rushing toward me. Small stones thudded and slapped against my legs and back but my clothing was thick enough to make it bearable, and at the bottom the universe saw fit to grant me a small favor, tumbling me into a thick patch of grass and fragrant mud that absorbed most of my momentum without breaking any bones.

I levered my body upwards and forwards, splashing into the river that I guessed was roughly knee-deep at this point, hoping that no rattlesnakes were swimming in here to escape the flames. Speaking of the inferno, I couldn't see as much from my new angle, just the angry orange light sweeping over the cliffs, accompanied by the freight-train roar of oxygen vaporizing. The water was cold but the riverbed was rocky, and I made quick progress across, trying to figure out where Frankie lay above me. If I went upstream a little further, I knew from my earlier observation, there was a spot where the cliff had crumbled into an angle of smaller boulders, and I could probably climb up to the trail there.

If the fire wasn't burning at that spot.

And if any gunmen in the dark didn't put a bullet through my head.

I had to try.

As I sloshed onto the bank, the fire above seemed to gain renewed speed, bright light boiling over the edge of the cliff. I was below but the smoke stung my eyes and the heat prickled my scalp. The flame-front would have reached where Frankie was lying. She might already be dead.

No, don't think like that.

She would have rolled off the cliff, into the water.

Unless she was too wounded to move.

Shit, get up there.

The rocks hot under my grip as I scrambled up the cliff, coughing ash.

The fire had moved beyond me, the wind jabbering in its wake. Bits of wood and burning grass swirled around my head. I scrambled over the edge of the cliff, wincing at the hot sand.

To my right, further up the trail, something amazing was happening.

The fire had intersected with a wide patch of rocks that acted as a natural firebreak, stopping it for the moment. Tongues of flame shot from a seething mass of gray smoke, shrinking as bushes and grass burned away. The wind had sparked smaller fires in the brush beyond, and those would likely gain size and speed within the next few minutes, but for now it seemed as if the firestorm had been checked.

"Daryl."

It was a croak, barely louder than the crackle of flames. A man stumbled out of the smoke. His black pants had burned mostly away, his bullet-resistant vest gray with ash. The fire had charred the right side of his head, leaving the skin a reddened, cratered mess. His left eye appeared fine, but the skin around the right had swollen and puckered over it. He seemed unarmed, too shocked to represent much threat.

"Who the hell is Daryl?" I asked, scanning the smoky cliffside for my sister.

"Daryl," the man said again, shaking his head. His blistered hands balled into fists, although I couldn't tell if that was reflex or he meant to hit me. I had no intention of killing a wounded man, but if he made any sort of aggressive move, I would put him down. Where was my sister?

The hard slap of a gunshot. The man's head jerked back, and he collapsed.

I ducked, spinning left. My sister emerged from the smoke, her hair charred, her eyes wide and crazed and very white in the sooty darkness of her face, her UMP socked to her shoulder.

"Thank God," I said.

"Thank Zippo," she said, passing me without breaking stride. The fabric of her shirt had burned away in patches, revealing pale skin beneath, and smoke rose from her shoulders in gray banners whisked away by the wind. I couldn't see any blood on her.

"What?" I reached out to touch her, but she shrugged my hand away. Whatever berserker energy had powered her insane run through flames and gunfire, killing everyone in her path, still coursed through her body.

"Fire pinned me down," she said. "So I knelt, used the Zippo, burned a little patch. Remember, *Young Men and Fire*? We talked about this?"

"I thought you were shot?"

"Grazed." She was picking up speed. "Keep up."

28

Frankie sprinted and I did my best to keep pace with her, flanking to her left, trusting that she knew her way up the treacherous path to the house, that she would avoid the flames chewing a bright line up the ridge before us, and every breath I took seemed loaded up with ash and blackened spores that settled deep in my lungs like handfuls of broken glass, prickly-painful against my ribs, and I fought the urge to stop and cough up my insides, my whole body feeling like a deflating bag of blood and piss, so exhausted, so drained, and Frankie was a deeper shadow against the night and smoke, silhouetted at moments by the flickering orange in front of us, and as the path rose toward the ridgeline she dodged to the left, guiding us through a gap between enormous stones, up the sharpest angle of cliff to the crest, and I heard a rustling before us that might have been the breeze rushing to feed the fire or it might have been a rattlesnake, the last thing I needed was poison in my veins and a swelling leg, not when we were miraculously still alive despite the firestorm and the bullets and the mercenaries, not when the house was so close, finally appearing up ahead—its white sides bright in the fire's flickering light, separated from us by thick smoke swirling with embers, and I caught Frankie waving her arm to the left, ordering me to create a little space between us, which I did, and not a moment too soon because the night to our right lit up, strobing white flashes, lead snapping past our heads as we ducked, Frankie already sighting and firing, bam, a liquid scream as a shadow crumpled, and instead of confirming the kill we kept running, the house looming larger now, gray smoke blurring out, and we needed a plan if we were going to survive the next five minutes, we needed to figure out which door to hit and how to move through the rooms beyond, but Frankie was locked into her rage, where all higher imaginings of tactics and strategy and stealth had given way before the pure need to kill, and when I pictured Janine in the upper rooms of the house I could feel that anger like a wildfire in my gut, consuming me, a bottomless fury that would ensure I killed everything in my path, that pumped fresh adrenaline by the bucket into my bloodstream, and I realized this was the best strategy, because the smoke from the fires cloaked us until we were on the lawn, and as we ran, to our left, in the driveway, headlights flashed on and men yelled, a team caught by surprise because the usual approach was to expect a cautious and careful enemy, and before anyone could pull a trigger, Frankie fired a burst at the back door, the knob shattering, and she was airborne and driving her knee into the wood and steel—painful as hell if we lived through this—and the door gave way, unlocked, smashing open to reveal the kitchen and two men looking up, surprised as Frankie, bouncing off the jamb, fired five times, the UMP tight against her chest, the gunshots deafening, the bullets shredding the men open, and before they hit the floor Frankie was already pushing past, darting right into the dining room, another gunshot, and I caught up as a third man smacked into the table before sprawling to the carpet, and that was good, but we had to worry about that team outside hitting the front door, and I was about to yell to Frankie about heading upstairs when something smashed into my lower back—my traitorous momentum carrying me into one of the dining table chairs, which toppled under my weight, spilling me onto my stomach, and I started coughing then, my muscles and lungs and brain electric with pain—and in the doorway stood another one of these seemingly endless mercenaries, a smoking pistol in his hand, and he swung the weapon toward Frankie but she was faster with the UMP, not bothering to raise it as she spun, simply firing off a burst into the bastard's knee, and he fell backward, his finger twitching on the trigger of his pistol, sending a round into the ceiling, and Frankie ducked forward, pulling the trigger again but she clicked on an empty chamber, and on reflex she ejected the magazine and slapped her leg pocket for a new one only to find it empty, and meanwhile I was trying to raise to my feet but my legs were weird, rubbery, my knees refusing to work, and looking down I saw a spreading mess of red above my hip, God, and I plucked at my shirt, seeing the graze through the tear in the fabric, not deep, and Frankie yelling at me to come on, come on, and the man on the floor was yelling something, cursing at Frankie, calling her all sorts of terrible things as she stepped to him—stepped *on* him, driving her ash-caked boot into his face hard enough to implode the nose into the skull—and then stooped and plucked his pistol from the floor and fired through the dining room doorway at the front door, which had crashed open, revealing a chaos of men and guns, and I ducked low as I scrambled past Frankie's feet toward the other bodies, retrieving what looked like a modified AR-15 with some kind of fiber forearm, a real science fiction weapon with an extended clip, which I emptied through the front door—men screaming, men dying—and as I clicked empty Frankie was moving, moving, moving through the front hallway and up the stairs to the upper floors, and here was the dangerous part, a stairway was where they always boxed you in, but we charged up and into the upstairs hallway and through the first door to the left, the bathroom filled with a pile of Frankie's men, shredded and dead, and Frankie unleashed a banshee scream of pure rage as she moved down the hallway and kicked open the door to the bedroom and then time stopped—

29

Janine sat on the floor beside the bed, pale, her hands on her knees, her fingers tapping a fast rhythm. Across from her, in a plush chair upholstered in blue fabric, sat Boz, his legs crossed, an MP5 submachine gun resting on his knee. The barrel of the weapon pointed in the general direction of Janine's head, and Boz's finger rested lightly on the trigger.

In the far corner of the room, beyond the bed, stood Jim. He had clearly chosen that spot on the assumption that it was the least likely place for him to catch a stray bullet through a window or door. He looked afraid, and I felt an absurd pang of sympathy for him. He had spent his adult life as a cop, but this was probably the biggest gunfight he'd ever seen.

Frankie pointed her pistol at Boz's head. I leveled my rifle at Jim, who flinched. I noted the pistol in his right hand, its barrel pointed at the carpet, his trigger finger resting on the slide. He clearly wanted no part of this, and that was good.

Frankie, breathing hard, said: "Who else is on this floor?"

Boz shrugged. "Just us, babe. I think you killed everyone else."

"Those shots before."

"They were killing your men." He shook his head. "I told Karen not to, but she insisted. Said they were criminals who deserved what they were getting."

"The guys who killed my guys," Frankie said, her voice almost strangled with rage. "Were they your guys?"

Boz shook his head. "Karen's. Some kind of executive protection firm."

"Fuck." Her weapon never wavering, Frankie jutted her chin ever so slightly in Janine's direction. "Janine, stand slowly and walk toward us."

Boz shook his head, and the barrel of his weapon swung an inch to the left, tight on Janine. My wife looked at me, her body almost shaking with hope and fear, and it took all of my self-control to not shoot Boz in the face. They tell you in training that a high-velocity bullet fired through the philtrum, that space between the top of the lip and the bottom of the nose, will travel through the skull and sever the brainstem before an assailant can pull a trigger or flip a switch. I'd seen a handful of people try that move over the years and it never worked out, the bullet always dipped or rose and left the attacker capable of squeezing in their last moment.

Boz shifted his gaze from Janine to me. "Hey, it's my almost brother-in-law."

"Don't you call him that," Frankie said. "Don't you dare. Where's Karen?"

"Out front, last anyone checked." Boz glanced at Jim. "That right, partner?"

Jim shrugged, his collar soaked in sweat.

"Tell you what," Boz said. "I really, really want to walk out of here alive. I got some prime weed at home, plus I was halfway through *The Nice Guys* when Karen called me in, and I really want to see how that shit ends."

"Nobody's stopping you," Frankie said. "Put the rifle down and walk on out."

"Ah, but how do I know you won't kill me?" Those dead eyes locked on me again. "Or him, considering I'm holding his wife hostage?"

"Because I'm only interested in Karen," Frankie said. "You're just…"

"Yeah, I'm not convinced." Boz spoke to Janine: "Maybe

you should come with me, honey. I'll drop you off a couple miles from here, or something."

If he tried walking out of here, I would try something. It would be stupid and risky, but not as stupid and risky as letting this man disappear with my wife.

"I don't think so," I said.

Against the wall, Jim shook. "Don't you dare," he told Boz. "Karen..."

A flash through the windows: headlights piercing the darkness, rumbling up the long dirt road to the house. I tensed. Did Karen call for reinforcements? What if this was the cops? But Jim looked out the window, and nothing I would have expected—relief, curiosity—flashed across his face. Instead, he seemed confused.

The headlights resolved into two SUVs braking hard in front of the porch. The passenger-side door of the first one opened, and the Monkey Man sprinted out, a rifle held at port arms. I had never been happier to see that lunatic in my life.

Jim's hand flexing on the pistol as he said to Boz: "We shouldn't have pulled those fucking men from the road." He sounded tired, resigned to whatever was about to happen.

"Excuse me all to hell, the attack was coming from behind," Boz said, looking at Frankie again. "How about one for the cider garden?"

Frankie's face shifted between narrow-eyed suspicion and something else—a warmth, a love that she had once held for this man. "Okay, fine." She lowered the pistol. "You walk out of here. Better go out the back."

Jim white-knuckled his weapon. "Boz, if you..."

Before any of us could react, Boz shifted the rifle, his finger tightening on the trigger. The explosion was loud in the confines of the room, rattling the windows. Janine screamed. Jim thumped hard against the wall behind him and slid to the floor, his eyes rolling back in his head, leaving a wide smear of red that did nothing to improve the wallpaper.

Boz set the smoking MP5 on the carpet and stood. As he walked past Frankie, he bent and whispered into her ear: "I loved you."

"I loved you, too," Frankie said, her fingertips grazing his cheek. "Now get out of here before I change my fucking mind. Avoid the fires."

"Oh, and one other thing," Boz said, pointing over his shoulder. "Karen, that cowardly bitch, is actually hiding under the bed."

30

The first shot punched through the bedspread, missing Janine's head by inches as I yanked her back. The second smashed the doorjamb, spraying wood and paint chips across the carpet. The third caught Boz behind the ear, driving him into the hallway, his forehead bouncing off the wall.

Frankie ducked and emptied her weapon into the gap beneath the bed, shattering the frame. Over the ringing in my ears, I heard a high-pitched scream of fear and pain.

A smoking pistol skidded from under the bed and thumped to a stop beside the chair.

"I surrender," Karen shouted.

Dropping to my knees, I found myself face-to-face with our tormenter, miraculously alive despite Frankie pounding at least three bullets in her direction. She had her well-manicured hands raised near her face. "Unarmed," she kept shouting. "I am unarmed. Unarmed, okay?"

Gripping one of her arms, I dragged her into the light. One of Frankie's bullets had grazed her cheek, leaving a streak of blood. Wasn't this always the way with high-value targets? They ordered so many people to their deaths, but when the time came, they were usually cowering in a closet or under a bed. Karen was no different than some terrorist emir.

Pounding on the stairs behind us. The Monkey Man appeared in the doorway, in his customary jumpsuit and mask, holding an UMP. Touching Frankie's shoulder, he said, his voice muffled by a layer of rubber: "Darling, you're hurt."

The world-shattering surprise of finally hearing the Monkey Man speak was lost in my heart-galloping fear when I saw the shiny darkness spreading across Frankie's shirt. "I know," Frankie said, swallowing hard, her forehead pale and speckled with sweat.

"Money," Karen said from the floor. Her expression was serious, focused somewhere above our heads. "I can give you all the money you want. All the connections. And we'll forget all this happened, of course…"

Looking down at her frightened and bleeding form, I flashed back—boom—to a long-ago night in Sadr City, Baghdad, when we finally brought down Hani Raja al-Tikriti, who headed a terrorist cell that had blown up a couple dozen people. I had been primary through the door, and as al-Tikriti raised his AK-47, I shot him twice in the stomach and once in the chest. As he lay on his living room carpet, dying, he shouted all kinds of things about God and forgiveness. I had no sympathy for the bastard, but at least he had tried to reach for something larger than himself in his final moments.

Karen, on the other hand, kept babbling about her bank account and hooking us up with only the best people.

Her hands trembling, Frankie shoved away the Monkey Man's hand. "Take me to the doc after this," she said, speaking very fast, spit bubbling on her lips. I realized she was speaking to me, not her lieutenant. "His name's Raylan and his address is in my phone. Code eight-two-three-five. There's money for him behind the living room wall…"

"Why are you telling me this?" I asked.

Frankie raised her pistol and shot gibbering Karen once between the eyes. "Because I'm about to pass out," she said, before collapsing bonelessly into the Monkey Man's arms.

PART 4
EXIT

31

The doctor, Raylan, was a tan, long-boned man who lived on a farm a few miles south of Frankie's safe house. His "doctor's office" was a windowless barn a hundred yards behind the main farmhouse, and it came with a small operating theater and a recovery room painted an aggressively annoying shade of pink.

While Raylan operated, the Monkey Man drove off to make sure the scene at the safe house was scrubbed. The men he'd brought with him had orders to remove the cash and weapons from the walls, then let the wildfire consume the building and the bodies inside it.

Janine and I sat on a small, crumbling bench outside of the medical barn, not saying anything, only focusing on the warmth of our hands and our breath hissing in the predawn cold. At my feet sat a duffel bag overstuffed with cash. We had taken fifteen shrink-wrapped blocks of hundred-dollar bills from the dining room wall before the high-speed drive to Raylan's farm. I figured that much cash would see us through the rest of this little adventure, with enough left over to pay for a year of our little girl's college education.

I also had a 9mm pistol in that bag. You never knew when new weirdness might erupt.

After an hour, Raylan appeared in the doorway, waving for me to follow him into the barn's front annex, which featured a sink, several cabinets, and a couple of waiting room chairs. He was still dressed in his surgeon's garb, smeared and dotted with blood.

"How is she?" I asked.

"We'll see," Raylan said, snapping his bloody gloves into the nearest trash can. "Bullet hit the upper border of the scapula, went through, but didn't penetrate the thoracic cavity. Another inch lower and it would have wrecked her lung."

I realized my fist was pressed to my mouth. Lifting it away, I flexed my tingling fingers. "Okay. I mean, that's a start, right?"

"If we were in a regular hospital, with all the tests you'd find there, I'd have a much clearer prognosis for you." Turning to the sink, Raylan washed his hands beneath scalding-hot water. "As it stands, I just don't know. If we're lucky, she'll have internal contusions, heal up pretty quickly. If we're not..."

"What's unlucky look like?"

"Clots." Raylan focused on scrubbing beneath his nails. "Unexpected complications. She shouldn't move for as long as possible. How long can she rest?"

I pictured the safe house burning like a funeral pyre, filled with charred skulls. How long until the cops arrived to sort through the carnage? Would they connect anything to us?

"I don't know," I said. "I think we have some breathing space, though."

Slapping the faucet off, Raylan dried his hands on a paper towel from the dispenser above the sink. "Okay. I can let her recover here, but it won't be free."

"Fine."

Now he looked at me, his blue eyes icy and unyielding. "The cost will reflect my risk in all this."

"Fine, yes, I understand."

"I have a police scanner in the house. I hear anything about the cops coming too close, she's out on her own. There's an access road, follows the river, not on the maps. You'll have to take her that way. I'll keep an eye on that big fire up the road, too, but I doubt it'll get close to here."

"I said I understand."

"Okay, as long as we're clear. It's a thousand a night, in advance, five days minimum." From the way his mouth set in a sharp line, he expected me to panic at that figure, maybe try to bargain him down.

Instead, I offered him my sunniest smile. "Fine. You have somewhere we can sleep, too? Me and my wife?"

He shrugged. "Can't let you in the main house. I'm sorry if that comes off as rude, but it's good security. Someone shows up unexpectedly, sees you, it's a problem. But there's a cot in the closet of Frankie's room. Big enough for you, if you squeeze. You okay with that?"

"More than okay. Thank you." I pried two stacks of cash from the duffel and slapped them onto the seat of the nearest chair. "Five days. Plus a little extra for food and whatever else."

Raylan thumbed through the cash, lips moving slightly as he counted it. "Where'd it come from?" he said.

"Not your business. It still spends."

"Yes, it does. Sorry, I've been a criminal doctor for years, so I know not to ask. But I can't help myself." Cradling the money stack like a baby, he headed for the door. "You need anything else, just call, okay? I should be awake for another hour or two."

"Thank you."

With a final nod, Raylan disappeared through the front door. I stood there and counted to fifty in my head, then searched the room, starting with the cabinets beneath the sink. More than anything I wanted to check on my sister, listen to her breathe, feel the warmth of her hand, but first I needed to take care of some things.

The sink cabinets offered alcohol wipes, tongue depressors, and bandages in shrink-wrapped boxes, along with bottles of rubbing alcohol and hydrogen peroxide. Nothing unusual, in other words: no hidden weapons or listening devices. I shut the cabinets and opened the paper towel dispenser. Nothing weird in there, either.

The shelving on the far side of the room, beyond the examination table, offered more of the same: bottles of medicines, boxes of medical supplies. The bottom tier featured two oversized cabinets with steel lids, the keys in the locks. I opened both, revealing folded towels and surgical gowns. Perfect.

I emptied the contents of the left cabinet, then stuffed the duffel bag inside and locked it. Pocketed the key. It was a cheap lock and no doubt easy to break, but it would allow me to leave the money in a relatively safe place while I completed my next task. After setting the pile of towels and gowns on a corner of the examination table, I stuffed the backup 9mm down the back of my jeans, covering the grip with the hem of my shirt, and went outside.

"Where you going, babe?" Janine asked.

"Back in a minute," I said.

Since we left the safe house, she had seemed pretty calm: no tapping, none of the repetitive behaviors that marked a hardcore OCD episode. I was so proud of how she had acted on the hostage video, refusing to back down in a room full of men with guns. Out of all of us, she was the one who seemed to have come through all of these recent troubles the strongest.

The wind picked up, rustling the tall grass. In the distance, what sounded like a loose piece of metal banged slowly, rhythmically. I paused, letting my eyes adjust as much as possible to the moonless night. No lights from the direction of Raylan's house. In any case, I didn't feel the telltale tingle of someone spying on me.

I sniffed deeply, trying to detect smoke. Nothing. No brightness on the horizon, either, of a wildfire out of control. I hoped it was contained. After it burned down the safe house to the foundation, that is.

I walked to the rear of the barn, making a mental note to count my steps in case I ever needed to do this again in the dark. When I reached the far end of the building, I patted the wall until my fingers ran over a doorjamb. If this wasn't the door I glimpsed in the back of Raylan's operating room when we brought Frankie in, it surely led to it.

Kneeling, I pulled out my phone and flicked it on, sweeping it along the ground in front of me. I'd never seen behind this particular barn before, but I'd lived in the West my whole life, so I knew that the backside of barns tended to accumulate all sorts of junk: piles of worn-out tires, old boxes, broken-down engine parts, and much more. On the far side of the door, Raylan or his employees had stacked plastic milk crates, filled with frayed hoses and rusted bits. The phone's weak glow played over dry weeds sprouting through the crates' grated sides. Nobody cleaned back here regularly. Good.

Letting the phone click off, I drew the 9mm from my waist-band and slipped it into the three-inch gap between the crates and the barn wall, the grip pointed toward the door. I stood, wiping my palms on my jeans, and thought: be prepared. Someone takes us hostage inside, tries to move us this way, I got a chance at grabbing another gun.

You're avoiding your sister.

That was true, too, as much as I hated to admit it. Stashing the money and the gun, exploring the exciting worlds of Raylan's medical cabinets—every minute I burned on those tasks was another minute I could put off entering the room where my sister lay wounded. Because as much as I loved her, if she was dying, I didn't think I could handle that. I needed time to prepare.

I needed her to wake up, so we could talk.

If she woke up, that is.

32

But Frankie kept sleeping.

While I sat beside her bed, I checked my phone over and over again. According to every news site, Karen had died in a tragic fire in eastern Oregon. The other dead men went unmentioned. Given the extreme remoteness of the site, it was probably easy for the state authorities to restrict access to the media.

Early the next morning, Raylan checked in and pronounced Frankie's vitals good. He shook her uninjured shoulder, and she groaned before sinking back into deep sleep. "If she doesn't come around by noon," he said, handing me a large paper cup of hot coffee, "come get me."

I nodded, grateful for the caffeine after the sleepless night. Once he left the barn, I stood and stretched my legs. The operating theater was still a mess, the floor littered with crumpled bandages soaked with Frankie's blood. I tried the door at its far end, the one that I assumed led to the outside, and found myself in a narrow hallway lined with large boxes of linens, glass jars for canning, and kitchen machines. How many hustles did Raylan have going on?

At the far end of the hallway, another door. This one led to the back of the barn, as I'd predicted. The pistol was still tucked away behind the crates, nicely hidden in shadow. I sipped my coffee and took a deep breath, willing the cold white sun to fill me with fresh energy. Maybe it was the lack of sleep, or the hours sitting in that hard chair beside Frankie's bed, but my body had started to ache, especially my thighs and lower back where I had collided with the rocks during my tumble down the canyon. When I went back inside, I would need to scrounge up whatever painkillers Raylan had left lying around, but I had a slightly more urgent task at hand.

When I circled back to the front of the barn, Janine was in a yoga pose, her face turned to the sun. Without looking at me, she asked: "Are we safe?"

"Yes."

"Swear to me."

"We are."

She sighed. "I love you."

"I love you, too."

"Frankie okay?"

"She will be, yeah." I forced as much optimism into my voice as I could.

A long pause. "Okay."

"Okay."

"So what now?"

"Normal life."

She snorted. "Whatever that means."

I wasn't interested in a fight. "Whatever that means," I said evenly.

"Can we go home? Get our kid?"

"Soon as we get Frankie out of here, yeah. Everyone who can hurt us is dead, I think."

My warrior woman laughed softly. "I love you, babe."

"I love you, too."

33

Back in the room, I took Frankie's hand and squeezed.

She squeezed back, startling me. Her left eye opening now, bloodshot, studying me with the intensity of a cat circling its prey. "Hey, bro," she said.

"Hey yourself."

"We good?"

I squeezed harder. "I hope so. I so hope so."

34

"You're going to hate me," Frankie said, bracing her hands on the edges of the bed, her jaw tightening.

"Don't you dare," I replied, rising from my seat because I already guessed what she had in mind. After opening her eyes for the first time, she had spent the past half hour lying in bed, not speaking. I'd left her to her thoughts, obsessively flicking through news sites on my phone. The few new articles still told the tale of Karen tragically killed in that fire, with no mention of all those other men. Was that a good or bad sign?

Ignoring my warning, Frankie locked her fingers around the bed's metal edges, set her elbows, and pushed with all her might, levering her body upright. The way her face paled, and a muscle in her jaw flexed, suggested it took nearly all her strength to make that move, but make it she had. "See?" she said. "I got this."

I was out of my seat, hovering over her. "Come on, lie back down."

"No." Her hands, light as birds, batted me away. "You sit back down."

I stepped away. "Don't tell me you're going to try and walk."

"There's no 'try' in this dojo, bro." Swinging her legs over the side of the bed, she paused to take a breath. "How was Raylan?"

"Little weird. But you know what he wasn't weird about? His belief that you got to stick in that bed a little longer."

181

"I feel fine."

"Bullshit."

"Well, I've been hit worse, how's that?"

"Also bullshit."

"Whatever." She straightened her arms, putting her weight on her hands, her legs swinging in space. If she tried to heave off the bed, I was prepared to catch her if she fell. She thought better of it, settling back with her chin on her chest, breathing deep and loud.

"You want some painkillers?" I asked.

"I want to walk," she said, but remained in place. "Any pursuit?"

"We might actually be in the clear." The last time Raylan had visited, to change Frankie's bandages, I had taken him aside and asked if he'd heard anything on the police scanner. Raylan said no, nothing, wasn't it weird?

"I'll believe it...when I see it." This time she grunted, and pushed, and before I could react, she was upright on quaking knees. She almost fell, so I slipped an arm around her waist, holding her up as I tried to lift her back into bed.

She slapped me on the back of the head. "Let me go," she growled in my ear. "I have to do this."

"Fine." I said, releasing her waist and stepping back. Let her fall. That might finally teach her the lesson.

"Watch. Me. Walk." This time Frankie shoved herself away from the bed, tottering across the room like the world's biggest toddler, grunting as she did so.

"Hey, it's alive," Janine called through the open doorway.

"Glad to see you, too," Frankie said, before turning her head toward me, to better whisper in my ear: "What about Boz?"

I pressed her close to me. "I'm so sorry, hon."

For the first time since we were kids, I saw a tear roll down Frankie's cheek. Like water coming to the desert after a long drought. Her chest hitched, and she winced: "Damn, that's painful." Whether she was referring to her healing wounds or her dead ex-boyfriend, I couldn't tell.

"I'm sorry," I said again.

"Imagine if I'd said 'yes' to kids," she said, keeping her voice low as we continued our march around the room. "Can you imagine? But still...that kid would have been terribly loved."

We stopped beside her bed, and she placed a hand against my chest. Her face turned away from mine, her hair a curtain over her eyes. In the new silence, her breath was slow, controlled, and full of razor-sharp pain.

"Would you like me to leave?" I asked.

"Yes. Please do."

35

Later that night, Janine and I perched yet again on the bench, finishing off a six-pack of beers provided by Raylan, who did a good job of pretending to care about our well-being. Janine still seemed happy, and I was increasingly convinced she wasn't pretending—a massive weight seemed to have lifted from her shoulders, along with the need to tap, to repeat, to work through her usual routines. Maybe it was temporary, but at this point I would take whatever I could get.

"It's funny." Janine placed her empty beer can on the gravel between her feet, then tried to stomp it flat. Her foot descended at the wrong angle, denting the side of the can, which toppled over. "Actually, *that* is funny. No, seriously, I've been doing a lot of thinking since we've been trapped here."

"We're not trapped," I said. "We can leave anytime we want."

"Sorry, we're in a holding pattern, I stand corrected." Janine said. "If I may continue, I had a bit of revelation a couple hours back. You and me, we spend our lives so worried all the time..."

"We do fine," I said, a little sharply. Usually I could down a couple of beers without effect—the benefits of a life of heavy drinking—but the exhaustion and terror of the past week had left me weakened, and my head was starting to spin.

"Yes, we do. And you do your part, unlike so many of my friends' asshole husbands. You don't know how grateful I am about that. But we worry, because that's, like, the human condition: the bills never end, the repairs never end, the issues never end. And I let all that stuff get into my head. I let it wreck me every day, whether or not I was showing it."

"We all show it, sometimes."

She took my hand. "I know. And then all this crap happened— the kidnapping, the incident in the woods, all that horrible stuff at the house—and you'd think I'd be more wrecked than ever. That I'd be tapping my knees and doorknobs and everything else to oblivion. But you know what happened?"

She must have been reading my thoughts. "You've seemed... relaxed," I said.

"Well, not exactly relaxed. But I feel like I'm calmer than I've ever been in years. Because we've endured some of the worst shit that the world can throw at us, and we're still here. We made it through. And if we've done that, then there's nothing we can't beat."

"Hell of a therapy."

"Yeah, we could totally market that. 'Near Death Therapy.' We could charge a fortune." Janine giggled, and I started to laugh, outsized peals from deep in my gut.

"Hundred bucks an hour," I said, once I'd sucked down enough oxygen to speak. "I could quit chasing scumbags. We'd take our clients, tie them up..."

"...chase them through the woods..."

"...fire a few shots over their heads..."

"...heck, set off a few explosions..."

"...and then, for an encore, we'd set their house on fire." I stopped laughing. "What's that?"

Headlights bloomed beside Raylan's farmhouse. An SUV creeping forward. No red-and-blue lights, no sirens. No way it was hostile, right? Any fragments of the Bakers' shattered empire would have snuck up on us with night-vision goggles and rifles, taking us down before we knew they were there.

Even so, I pictured the pistol tucked behind the barn, and regretted how it wasn't in my waistband. I was tempted to tell still-giggling Janine to head inside, but something told me this was okay.

The SUV flashed its lights as it closed in, drawing to a stop fifteen feet away. The Monkey Man climbed out, a small blue backpack in his left hand. I offered him a nod, which he returned before disappearing inside the barn.

"We should also think about redoing the bathroom," Janine said, as if a man with a rubber chimp mask hadn't just walked past. "Maybe repainting the first floor. I know you have a lot going on, but what do you think?"

"Not the worst idea. I've been wanting to redo the shed, too," I offered. "Fresh start, get the old ghosts out."

"Wait." Janine gave me a look of mock surprise. "There are ghosts in the house?"

"You're right, a fresh start's a good idea."

The Monkey Man exited the barn, Frankie limping in his wake. She was dressed in jeans and a fresh T-shirt underneath one of her trademark black jackets, which made her bloodless face seem paler. While her lieutenant opened the SUV's rear hatch and tossed the backpack inside, she turned to us.

"Janine," she said. "Could you give me and my bro a moment, please?"

"Sure." Kissing me on the cheek, Janine stood and left.

"Where are you going?" I asked Frankie, nodding at the SUV. The Monkey Man was leaning against the front bumper, hands in his pockets, his masked chin against his chest. It was one of the few times I'd seen him without a weapon. In fact, he seemed almost relaxed. And if he could loosen up a bit, that might mean we had truly survived our recent troubles.

"Away for a long time," she said. "I'm thinking Mexico, maybe around Veracruz. I still know some folks down there."

"Why?" I tried to keep my voice under control. After everything we'd endured, how could she leave?

Frankie sighed and nodded toward the Monkey Man. "I've lost so many of my people. I used to think I was such a badass, and it was a great feeling—but after everything we've been through, now it feels like a matter of time until I get hit again. This time permanently."

"So this is a vacation." I smiled at her, trying to make light of it, although I knew that was the wrong response.

Frankie hissed through her front teeth. "I love you, bro, but you've always had a mouth on you."

I stopped smiling. "I'm sorry about Boz, if that means anything."

"I'm sorry that what he and I had is gone. But he chose the wrong side. Maybe so did I." She tugged my beard, lowering my head to her level. "But you didn't. You're the good one of us, even if you do make too many stupid comments. I need to go figure out who I'm going to be."

I removed her hand from my beard, held it. Her fingers were cold, and in the faint moonlight I saw my sister as the old woman she would probably never become: her skin wrinkled and paper-thin over dark veins, her bones so small and brittle. Then the illusion passed, as quick as a nighttime cloud, and she was young again, brimming with a dark energy that no bullet could extinguish.

"Take care of yourself," she told me.

"I always do."

Standing on tiptoes, she kissed me on the forehead, then walked for the SUV, never looking back. The Monkey Man climbed behind the wheel and started the engine, spinning the vehicle toward the farm's driveway. I stood and watched as their headlights shrank, flickered, and disappeared, leaving me to the night's humming silence.

ACKNOWLEDGMENTS

I never intended to write a sequel to *Boise Longpig Hunting Club*, which for the longest time spoke to me as a standalone novel. However, as more people read it—and let me know they'd read it, and enjoyed it—the more I began to hear Frankie and Jake in my head again. Even so, the sequel's plot didn't gel for the longest time; I wrote part of a draft that took place in New Orleans, another that involved completely different themes and characters, and so on.

So I set that mushy proto-manuscript aside. A couple months later, for reasons too convoluted to go into here, my wife and I were hiking around Three Forks, which is beautiful and rugged country in eastern Oregon. It is also remote and filled with rattlesnakes. We were on a quest for a beautiful set of hot springs cascading down the side of a cliff, which turned out to be stunning indeed—but reaching them required a slog down an overgrown trail, through tall grass and over rusted barbed wire, with a few unfortunate encounters with rattlers thrown into the mix. Our friend A. guided us through with encouragement… and by the time we made it back to the truck, dusty and exhausted, I had the seeds for Frankie and Jake's next, true adventure firmly planted in my mind. Thank you, A. It was all worth it.

My wife, as always, does more than she realizes for these books. No writer is an island, and I wouldn't be able to do what I'm meant to do without her.

I also want to thank Eric Campbell, Lance Wright, and the whole pirate crew at Down & Out Books, for sticking with these books from beginning to not-so-bitter end. As I bring this book to a close, I wanted to call out Chris Rhatigan, peerless editor, who beat this manuscript into its finest possible shape.

NICK KOLAKOWSKI is the author of the Love & Bullets Hookup series of crime novellas. His short fiction has appeared in *Thuglit, Shotgun Honey, Plots with Guns,* and various anthologies. His fiction and non-fiction have appeared in *The Washington Post, McSweeney's,* NPR's website, *The North American Review,* Shotgun Honey, *Thuglit, Spinetingler,* and other magazines and anthologies. He is the author of the noir novels *A Brutal Bunch of Heartbroken Saps* and *Boise Longpig Hunting Club* as well as the satirical nonfiction book *How to Become an Intellectual.* He lives and writes in New York City.

BOOKS

On the following pages are a few
more great titles from the
Down & Out Books publishing family.

For a complete list of books and to
sign up for our newsletter,
go to DownAndOutBooks.com.

Suicide Blonde
Three Novellas
Brian Thornton

Down & Out Books
October 2020
978-1-64396-044-9

Three Stories. Three Eras. Three Crimes.

A 1960s mob fixer is drawn into a Vegas fix that might just put the fix on him.

Dead Chinese immigrants wash up on the beaches of 1889 Seattle and one government official refuses to look the other way.

An Italian ex-galley slave, sometime thief, and full-time rogue masterminds a one-of-its kind jail break in 1581 Constantinople.

Don't Shoot the Drummer
A Lou Crasher Novel
Jonathan Brown

Down & Out Books
November 2020
978-1-64396-150-7

A security guard is murdered during a home robbery of a house tented for fumigation and Lou Crasher is asked to solve the murder. The rock-drumming amateur P.I. is up for it, because his brother Jake is the one asking. Lou fights to keep his musical day job and catch the killers.

When the bullets fly he hopes all involved respect his golden rule: Don't Shoot The Drummer.

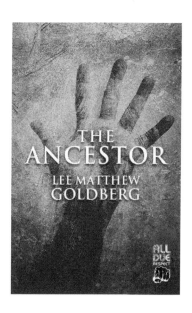

The Ancestor
Lee Matthew Goldberg

All Due Respect, an imprint of
Down & Out Books
August 2020
978-1-64396-114-9

A man wakes up in the Alaskan wilderness with no memory of who he is, except for the belief that he's was a prospector from the Gold Rush and has been frozen in ice for over a hundred years.

A meditation on love lost and unfulfilled dreams, *The Ancestor* is a thrilling page-turner in present day Alaska and a historical adventure about the perilous Gold Rush expeditions where prospectors left behind their lives for the promise of hope and a better future.

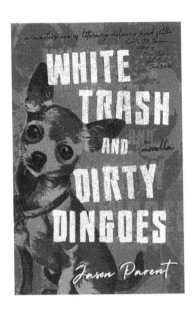

White Trash and Dirty Dingoes
Jason Parent

Shotgun Honey, an imprint of
Down & Out Books
July 2020
978-1-64396-101-9

Gordon thought he'd found the girl of his dreams. But women like Sarah are tough to hang on to.

When she causes the disappearance of a mob boss's priceless Chihuahua, she disappears herself, and the odds Gordon will see his lover again shrivel like nuts in a polar plunge.

With both money and love lost, he's going to have to kill some SOBs to get them back.

Printed in Great Britain
by Amazon